Praise for P

CW01460856

'Deliciously thrilling and wildly unpredictable'

– Oxford Today

'An authoritative style, a generous sprinkling of
recurring images and clues, and plenty of twists …
I couldn't put the book down until the end'

– Daily Information

'I was bamboozled by the solution to the puzzle and
needed to look through the book again to see how the
author pulled it off. Bravo!'

– Peter Lovesey, winner of three CWA Daggers

PETER
TICKLER
DEATH IN THE
SEA POOL

ISBN: 978-1-910779-51-4

Typeset and cover design
by Oxford eBooks Ltd.

Oxford eBooks

www.oxford-ebooks.com

DEDICATION / THANKS

Writing is a solitary business, but a writer needs other people to get the story out there. I would like to acknowledge: Helen Baggott for her editing skills; Dorothy Flaxman for checking the accuracy of my Bude; Andy of Oxford-eBooks for putting it all together (including the paperback edition); and my wife Fiona for her tolerance.

Of course, any errors in the text are my responsibility. I like my locations to be as accurate as possible, but as a writer I reserve the right to make stuff up when the story demands it.

CHAPTER ONE

IT WASN'T EXACTLY planned. It was more a case of one thing leading to another and then, quite suddenly, she was dead.

She had been huddling at the bus stop waiting for the rain to ease. Mick Raglan had stopped and asked if she was alright, and she had nodded and cadged a couple of cigarettes off him. Despite his rough appearance, he was a bit of a soft touch. All she had to do was flirt a bit and say how her mum never gave her money and the next thing was he was offering her two of his, one of which she tucked up her sleeve. She waited for him to light the other, and then took a long drag, before expelling her smoke straight into his face. He didn't react, and as she stood there, smiling, she wondered if he fancied her like some of the others clearly did.

'Can't even afford to buy a cheap lighter and a packet of ten,' she said, seeing how far she could push it. She waited for a response, and he had, after a moment or two of hesitation, handed over his own disposable lighter and two more cigarettes.

'That's all I've got,' he said, and she felt a slight – but only slight – twinge of guilt. Then she had headed off up the road, past Nanny Moore's footbridge and straight on up the slope until she reached the headland.

It had been his idea to meet her, but when she arrived he wasn't waiting for her. She felt a flash of irritation. They had agreed a time. If he thought he could mess her around just because she was fifteen, then he could think again. She would give him a couple of minutes and then that was it. She flicked on her torch. It wasn't completely dark, but she decided to go down to the pool to check it out. If he wasn't skulking down there, she would head for home. She could walk across the sand since the tide was out. At the bottom of the steps, she scanned the surrounding area with her torchlight. No-one! At least he wasn't playing silly buggers in the dark. She'd give him one more minute and then …

There was a noise behind her and she spun round as a light glared full into her face. She squealed in sudden panic.

He laughed and lowered the light so that it was shining on her lower half. 'It's only me.'

'Hell, you gave me a fright.'

The smile on his face faded. 'I thought it was about time we had a chat.'

'I think I made myself very clear.'

'You made yourself very clear, in particular that you are not a person to be trusted.'

'We agreed a deal. In the circumstances I don't think my price is out of order.'

'Little girls who play with fire end up getting burnt.'

'Have you got the money? Because if you have we'll call it quits. Water under the bridge. Maybe I'll even let you have another feel just to show you there no hard feelings.' She giggled.

'No hard feelings?' he growled.

'Or have you got them already?' More giggles as

she realised what she had said.

'Bitch!'

One moment she was laughing hysterically at her own joke, and the next she was lying on the ground. One moment full of life, and the next – to all appearances – dead. He stared down at her for several seconds, focusing his torchlight on her face. There was no sign of life. He picked up the large round stone which had smashed into her temple and tossed it out into the middle of the pool. Then, using just his feet, he rolled her over the edge into the water. He switched his torch on, playing it across her as she floated face down, arms outstretched, hair fanning out in the water. He switched off the torch and stood very still, listening. He looked up into the sky. The rain clouds parted, allowing a shaft of moonlight across the bay. It was time to go.

'It was someone else!'

They had both been silent until this point, apart from the initial cursory exchange of names. Not that there had been any real need for introductions. Doug Mullen knew all too well who Mick Raglan was, because he had been researching him intermittently over the last few days. And it was Raglan who had contacted him in the first place, asking him to come and meet him, so he had doubtless done his own research on him, in so far as he could from inside a prison hospital.

'I didn't kill her, I swear.' Raglan's voice was louder this time, with a rasp which betrayed anger, desperation and extreme ill-health.

Doug nodded, but said nothing. What was he meant to say to the man? 'I believe you.' Or maybe, 'I don't believe you.' But the fact was that he couldn't bring himself to say either of these things.

'Cat got your tongue?' Raglan snapped, sending a shower of spittle across his bed.

A nurse – or was she a prison warder in nurse's clothing – had been standing in the doorway observing the two men, and now she strode forward, arms swinging like pistons and feet thudding like she meant business. Her shadow fell ominously across Raglan's bed. 'Mick,' she growled with a thick Glaswegian accent. 'Any more of that, and I'll be asking your visitor to depart.'

'It's alright,' Doug said, ever the peace-maker.

'It's not alright,' she snapped back. 'I'm in charge here, and I say it is definitely not alright.' Doug felt the full force of her personality. 'Alright, mister?'

He nodded submissively. 'Alright.'

She stomped away and disappeared from view, as if satisfied that neither of them would now dare misbehave.

'She's cute, ain't she,' Raglan said. 'If I wasn't a complete ruddy wreck …' A burst of coughing stopped him in his tracks, so much so that Doug got up and handed him the glass of water on his side-table.

When he had recovered, Doug asked the obvious question. 'So you want me to prove that you're innocent?'

Raglan nodded, and lay back against his pillow. The fit had taken it out of him. Doug wondered how much longer he had. By the look of it, a month or two at most. But if so, why was he looking for someone to prove his innocence now?

'Lots of cons claim to be innocent,' Doug said quietly.

'You think I am lying? So how come you've turned up here today? Curious to see me, to get a close-up decko of a notorious convicted killer? Or maybe you're wondering how much I'm prepared to pay you? I expect it looks like easy money. You get a whack of cash, up front of course, and even if I die pronto, you will still go through the motions of pretending to investigate Layla Lark's death so you can collect the rest of the money.'

'Why me?' Doug said, ignoring the dig that he was only in it for the money.

'You came recommended. Old hatchet face knows your girlfriend apparently.'

'Ah!' Doug said as the penny dropped. How come Becca had never mentioned it? But then, how come he hadn't mentioned to her what he was up to today? Of course he knew the answer to that. Taking on a job which involved working for a convicted killer had made him feel decidedly queasy.

Raglan coughed again, this time less fervently. He held up his hand. 'I'm tired. The deal is three grand up front and three more if you collect enough evidence to force the authorities to reopen case. Take it or leave it. But for the sake of my daughter, I hope you take it. I don't want her to live the rest of her life thinking her dad was a killer. You're my – and her – last chance.'

'First, tell me about that evening, when Layla died.'

'I saw her at the bus stop. You must know that. I never denied it. It was all over the media. I gave her a fag. We chatted and then we parted.'

'Was she waiting for someone? Or maybe waiting for a bus?'

Raglan had collapsed back on his pillow and closed his eyes. Doug waited for him to recover and answer. He knew he would take the job on, but he didn't want to seem too eager, didn't want to give the impression – even to a man standing before the open door of death – that he was motivated by money. But the fact was that he and Becca had bought a small house and had mortgaged themselves up to the hilt. The money would be more than useful, especially now that Becca was pregnant.

Raglan didn't say anything more. He was breathing softly and regularly, seemingly asleep and maybe temporarily at some sort of peace.

The nurse-warder was back by the bed, bending down and checking her patient-prisoner's vital signs. 'No more questions. He needs to rest.'

'Tell him I'll take the job,' Doug said firmly. 'On the terms he offered.'

She gave him a bleak stare. 'I'll tell him. But, make sure you don't just take the money and run. He deserves better than that.'

Zoe Finch had no concrete sense of her father. The closest memory she had was of being carried on the shoulders of a man smelling of tobacco smoke, her hands holding tight to his soft curly hair. She had no remembrance of his face, not least because there had never been any photos of him in any of the houses in which she and her mother had lived. She had lost count of how many places they had called 'home'. They had never stayed anywhere very long, hardly ever long enough to begin to feel that this was a place she belonged, and certainly never long enough to make a best friend.

The first time they had upped sticks and gone – or rather the first time she could remember – she had come down the stairs for breakfast and found their cases standing neatly in the hall. Hers was pink, and her mother's matching pair were silver. There had been no time for breakfast, because a taxi had turned up and hooted outside the door before she had been able to get any cornflakes into her bowl. Then there had been a day of travelling on three – or maybe it was four – different trains until they arrived in a big town where everyone spoke with a very strange accent. Within a few days she was in another school, while her mother went off and earned money cutting women's hair. And in the evening she would sometimes cut the hair of men who knocked on her door with a smile on their face and a bag of sweets in their pockets. Those were for Zoe herself.

And that was how life was: moving on, settling, and then moving on again until the day that her mother went to work as usual and never came back. It was the police who came to the door that evening, just as Zoe was wondering where the hell she had got to and should she throw out the fish and chips which were lying cold and untouched on the table. She had bought them as a treat with the proceeds of her Saturday job in town. It was the female officer who had done the talking, explaining that someone who they believed to be her mother had been hit by a car down on the Blackpool Road and had been pronounced dead shortly after her arrival at the local A & E.

But if the death of her mother had not been enough of a shock, going through her mother's effects a few weeks later produced another one which transfixed her. Newspaper articles about a man called Mick Raglan, who had murdered a girl in Bude. Family snaps of him, on his own and with a woman who was quite clearly her own mother. And in one photo, a side-view shot, her mother was smiling happily at the camera, while Mick grinned proudly beside her. And the reason for the smile was obvious: a swollen stomach. Her mum was pregnant. And Mick Raglan was, surely, the expectant father. Her father.

Roxanne stood up at the top of the cliffs looking out across the sea. The days were longer now, and as long as she didn't waste any time at the end of her shift in the cafe, she had time to go home and get up onto the cliffs for a walk before it got too dark. It was cold, the wind cutting through her thin coat, but the sky was clear and that meant she could have a few more minutes there before turning for home.

Her mobile phone rang. She ignored it. They could leave her a message and she'd check it out in her own good time. If it was a cold caller, she'd block the number. There had been a spate of them over the last few weeks, and if you once answered them, they would never give you any peace.

Five minutes later, just as she had started to retrace her steps back down the hill, the phone rang again, but it was a different number, from Truro. She swore and answered it.

'Where have you been, Roxy?' She recognised the voice. It was Janet from the agency. She had never met her, but they had spoken a number of times. 'The new visitors are waiting outside Seagull Cottage and they can't get in. There's no key in the key-safe. What's going on?'

She felt in her coat pockets and immediately located it. She had used it to let herself in and out that morning when she had turned the heating on low to take the chill off the house. She had meant to put it back in the key-safe as she always did before new guests arrived, but for some reason she had failed to do so. 'I'm sorry,' she said. 'I'll be there in ten minutes and sort it out.'

'Make it five,' Janet snapped. 'And make sure you apologise or they'll end up giving us a rubbish review just because of your incompetence.'

'Of course,' she replied, but Janet had already killed the call.

Both Doug Mullen and Becca Baines were feeling a bit frazzled. It had been a long journey, with major jams on both the M4 and the M5, and when they arrived outside the cottage in Lynstone Road, Becca had been absolutely desperate to get to a toilet. But it was the dog, Rex, who had spent most of the journey happily lying at her feet, who was the first out of the car. He immediately located a good place under a squat holly tree to relieve himself, while Becca located the key-safe and discovered that the key was missing. 'Hellfire!' she exclaimed, and made a beeline round the back of the house. When she re-emerged a couple of minutes later, she was looking mighty relieved.

'I've rung the agency,' Doug said, and immediately followed suit. When he returned, he found her sitting on the low stone wall eating a bag of crisps, while Rex sat expectantly at her feet in his well-practised *feed me* pose.

'I could do with fish and chips when this is all sorted,' Becca said, just before she poured the residue of crumpled crisps straight into her open mouth.

Ten minutes later they were inside the cottage and the woman who let them in was clucking round them like a mother hen on steroids. 'I'm so sorry,' she said three times. 'I got distracted. It's been a difficult day. Can I ask you not to mention it on your report or I'll never hear the end of it. I need the work. My shifts in the cafe don't go far enough and—'

'Where's the best fish and chip place?' Becca cut in, the inconvenience of the missing key already consigned to the past. 'We're starving.'

'Here!' She picked up a folder of leaflets on the sideboard and passed it over. She pointed at one of the adverts. 'This is the best, if you ask me.'

Becca stared at the leaflet and sighed. She sat down.

'Do you mind if I ask when the baby is due?' the woman said.

A smile spread across Becca's face. Being asked about the baby was the perfect way to win her approval. 'Just had the twenty-week scan, so now is a perfect time for a break by the seaside.'

'Everything alright, sir?' She was aware that the man was silent and was reading the hand-written welcome sheet which she had left on the table that morning.

He looked up. 'Call me Doug. This is Becca. And you must be—?

'Roxanne.'

He frowned, uncertain how to proceed. 'Roxanne Lark?'

'Yes.'

'So … so … are you the mother of Layla?'

She stared at him speechless, and a frisson of alarm ran across her face. Becca forgot her baby, suddenly aware of the dangerous waters into which they had drifted.

Doug scratched at the stubble on his chin and vowed to himself that he would shave before he went to bed. 'I think it is only fair to tell you than I am a private investigator and have been hired by Mick Raglan to—'

He never finished his sentence because Roxanne opened her mouth, uttered nothing and then collapsed like a proverbial sack of potatoes onto the floor.

'So what do you think?' Becca said.

They had eaten their fish and chips in the house, but were now out walking along the canal towards the beach. Doug was glad to get some exercise and feel the fresh air in his lungs after too much of the day stuck in the car. By contrast Becca had been reluctant to exchange the warmth of the house for the chill outside air, and her pace was slow. It was a cloudless night, and above their heads a half-moon and a collection of stars and satellites decorated the sky.

'What do you mean?' Doug was tired after the drive, and his brain had been invaded by the fairies.

'What do you think I mean?' she replied sharply. She was tired too. 'The house. It's pretty damned odd that the house we are staying in is looked after by Layla's mother.'

'Not so much odd; deliberate, I'd say.'

'You mean Mick Raglan planned this all?'

Doug shook his head and winced. He had a low-grade headache and wished he had taken some paracetamol. 'I don't think he's well enough to have organised this, except maybe in his head. It must have been his daughter. She must have found out that Roxanne still lived down here and when she discovered that she looked after one or two holiday cottages, she must have deliberately booked this one for us so we were bound to meet her.'

'But didn't she warn you?'

'No.'

'Why ever not?'

He sighed. 'I've never met her. Your guess is as good as mine. Maybe she wanted to make sure I didn't just pretend to investigate.'

They had reached the end of the canal. Just beyond the heavy wooden lock gates the sand lay bright and enticing in the moonlight. They stood there silent, taking it in. But Becca had had enough. She pulled at his arm. 'Let's get back to the cottage, Doug. I'm ready for bed.'

CHAPTER TWO

JOSIE ARCHER HAD been sitting outside the front of the Weir restaurant, waiting for Doug to arrive, for fifteen minutes. She had herself arrived early, so he was only a couple of minutes late. Had she concentrated on the birds on the pond in front of her – mostly mallards and a couple of grebes, but including one statuesque heron – she might have distracted herself, but with every second that was passing her anxiety was rising. A waiter came out and, without actually saying anything, indicated with a tightening of his lips that if she was going to sit there and occupy a table, then the least she could do was order a coffee. Archer looked away.

It was stupid to have agreed to meet him. It was the last thing she wanted, and yet when he had rung her up and asked if he could talk to her about the murder of Layla, she had said 'Yes', barely pausing to think. Why shouldn't she? It was history now. What harm could possibly come of her answering a few questions? But now that she was here, at the cafe which she had suggested and wearing the checked coat and orange hat as she had promised, panic had begun to bubble up inside her. Her brain was having a volte-face. The last thing she wanted was to dredge up the past. Layla was dead, her killer was in prison, and that was all there was to it.

She looked at her watch again. He was now almost five minutes late. Maybe he wasn't coming. Maybe he was a crank. If he couldn't turn up on time, why should she wait? Maybe it was a sign from God. Layla had believed in signs, though not necessarily from God. Maybe this was just that – Layla or He Himself – telling her that she should never have come. It was a big mistake. She stood up sharply and began to walk away. She fiddled feverishly at the buttons on her coat. Now that she had made the decision, the sooner she got away, the safer she would be. She jammed her hat into her pocket and strode off down the slope, and headed for the path by the canal, oblivious of her ginger hair streaming out behind her. When she got home, she would draw down all the blinds, double lock the door, block his phone number, and hope he got the message.

She hurried on, head down, brushing past an elderly woman and pushchair. Twenty minutes of hard walking and she would be safely home. Stomp, stomp, stomp.

'Josie! Josie?' She glanced up and stopped dead. Some ten metres away a man was slowing to a halt. His face was red and his breathing was rushed. 'Are you Josie? I'm so sorry. It took longer than I expected and …'

'I think you must have confused me with someone else,' she said prissily.

'You're not Josie Archer?' He frowned and passed a hand across his forehead. 'But … but you are wearing a checked coat and unless I am mistaken that is an orange hat peeping out of your pocket.' He pointed, and then paused, waiting for a response which didn't come. Undaunted, he moved closer and held out a hand. 'I'm Doug Mullen. I can show you my driving licence if you wish. I …'

'I've changed my mind about talking to you.' She wanted to sound definite, inflexible, a woman not to be trifled with, and yet she sensed that she sounded none of these things.

'Of course.' He nodded vigorously. 'I cannot insist you speak to me, nor would I want you to speak to me against your will, but I do hope that you might at the very least listen to what I have to say.' He paused, allowing his breathing to slow down. 'Perhaps I can buy you one of Cornwall's famous cream teas?' He smiled. 'My treat, of course, and while I explain myself, you might be kind enough to put me right on whether I should put the cream on first and then the jam, or vice versa?'

'That was a rubbish chat-up line,' Josie said ten minutes later, after the two cream teas had been delivered to their table. 'Cream or jam first?' she clarified. Up until that moment, she had said nothing except rather gracelessly agreeing that she would accept his offer of a free tea.

'I wasn't trying to chat you up.'

'You know what I mean.'

'Point taken.' He watched her as she took a scone and put it on her plate, then poured herself a cup of tea. He cleared his throat. 'I wasn't expecting you to do a runner.'

'Who said I was doing a runner? You were late. I decided you were just some unreliable creep.'

'I thought maybe you were having a bit of a panic about talking to me. It would be perfectly understandable. I can imagine that remembering poor Layla might bring back all sorts of difficult memories.'

'Let's eat first,' she said. 'I'll show you how it's done.' She cut the scone on her plate in two before smearing clotted cream on each half and then jam. She took a bite. Doug followed suit. She studied him, and smiled as she saw a blob of cream escape from the corner of his mouth. She pointed her knife at him and laughed. 'Gotcha! I was born in Devon. Moved here when I was six.'

Only when their plates were empty and they had both replenished their teacups did she allow him to 'do his spiel'.

'You make me sound like a double-glazing salesman.'

'No offence intended.'

'None taken.'

She listened intently to what he had to say, about Mick Raglan's health and his desperate insistence that he had not killed Layla. Doug admitted that he had at first been sceptical, but had become convinced that Raglan might be telling the truth. 'I stress the word "might",' he added quickly. He didn't want to lose her cooperation. 'Killers can be devious and clever, but, rightly or wrongly, I decided to give him the benefit of the doubt and look at the case again.'

He paused, wondering how she would react. She jumped in. 'I reckon you're a soft touch, Mr Mullen. A court found him guilty. And no-one down here believes otherwise. To be honest, it's a part of this town's history that everyone would like to forget. I saw him smoking with Layla in the bus stop down by the river that evening, and no-one else saw her again after that. The bastard had a bit of a reputation with the girls. There was other evidence too, and it all pointed to him.'

'I've read all the media reports,' Doug said softly. 'And I can understand how people might feel about him. But the fact is that when he says he didn't do it, when he asks me to investigate even though his own death is staring him in the face, then I am inclined to take him seriously.'

'But you're being paid, right? You're a private investigator, so you only investigate when someone pays you. Nothing for nothing, right?' Her voice was sharp now, laden with venom, spitting out the words like they were the sourest of fruit.

Doug picked up his cup and drained it. He put it down and looked straight into her brown eyes. 'Yes, I am being paid. Mick Raglan wants me to prove that he is innocent. What I want to do is find out the truth. Maybe those two things will turn out to be the same thing.'

She stood up and began to button up her coat. 'I've got to go.'

He took out a business card, scribbled an address on the back and offered it to her. 'This is where I am staying. I'll be here for a couple of weeks. Josie, I do hope you will feel able to help me.'

She took the card, and studied it for several seconds, front and back. Then she tore it into four pieces and threw them into the wind. 'Mr Mullen, please don't ring me again,' she said before storming off into the weather.

He watched her go, her coat flying out behind her, hat jammed firmly down over her hair. He sighed and poured himself the remainder of the tea. It was now strong and more bitter than he liked, but he swallowed it nevertheless. He didn't like waste. Down below, the heron which had been standing, one-legged and motionless, on the far side of the lake, suddenly opened its wings and rose into the air, swinging with cumbersome grace towards Bude. Like Josie, it had had enough of Doug's company.

Andy Trent fought his way up Bude's main street, pushing on his wheels relentlessly with the smooth precision which he had used when he'd been into rowing. Judy had once tried to get him to buy an electric powered wheelchair, but he had turned it down in no uncertain terms. She had secretly arranged for a guy to come round to their house with his 'latest model' in the back of his van. Andy had soon seen the guy off, with his tail between his fat little legs, and then had a blazing row with Judy.

'I'm not a bleeding invalid. I can push myself round this piddly little town. So don't you ever do that again. Do you hear me?'

Judy had heard all right. She had disappeared to her mother's for two days, and only came back when he turned up at her mother's flat and apologised. It had taken him more than an hour of hard labour to get there, and he had arrived in a muck sweat and with a bunch of cheap flowers on his lap. Maybe it was the effort involved which had won Judy over, rather than the rather pathetic bunch of wilting gerbera which he had handed over to her and which she left behind in a vase for her mother. She had walked all the way home with him, pushing her bike alongside him, and later they had repaired the damage with fish and chips looking out at the sea – and later some unusually energetic sex.

But Andy wasn't thinking about this. That was water under the bridge, best forgotten – except for the sex. Instead he was thinking about the startling news he had just received from his daughter Naomi. She had sneaked out the back of the hair-dressing joint where she worked to ring him, but a combination of the strengthening wind and someone's chainsaw antics made it difficult to work out what she was saying. Nevertheless he had got the gist and that had been enough to dial his heart rate up several notches. Some private eye was in town asking questions about Layla Lark. That had all been fifteen years ago, and Mick Raglan had been done for it. All over and done with. But when Andy stopped at the top of the slope for a breather, he realised he was shaking. Layla and Mick, it was as if two ghosts had walked back into Bude. And he had no doubt that if this Mullen fellow was any good, he'd soon be knocking on his door asking damn-fool nosy questions about the pair of them, and no doubt himself too. It had been bad enough at the time. The whole affair had sent him into a spiral of drink, and after that had come the car crash and the amputation of his left leg, plus a prison sentence because of the young woman whose life he had ruined. But Judy had refused to give up on him. They had had their ups and downs since then, but he hadn't touched the booze since he got out, and Judy remained the best thing that had ever happened to him. He didn't want any private eye digging up skeletons and messing that up.

They walked steadily across the sand. It wasn't busy. The season and the visitors hadn't yet arrived, the school kids were apparently all at home playing on their gaming consoles or doing all the things they like to do on social media. There were the dog walkers of course, braving the chill wind off the sea, and a couple of women in wetsuits walking determinedly towards the waves with their surf boards.

Becca had slowed down markedly in the last week or so. Doug had noticed this, but had been wise enough not to comment. There was no rush today. The tide was barely on the turn, leaving plenty of time to amble across to the sea pool and then return before the sea came in and forced them to take a much more circuitous route inland. He wanted to see where Laura had died. He didn't think he would gain any insight into what had happened all those years ago. In fact he was pretty sure that he would not. But he knew he had to pay it a visit, and to acknowledge the sadness and tragedy of her death.

When they reached the pool, they climbed up the steps and stopped, looking in silence across the water. The surface moved uneasily as the wind gusted erratically across it, but Doug found himself unable to look directly into the pool. He was gripped by the thought that if he did, he might see her float to the surface, not like the Lady of Shallot in the painting –

he had seen enough dead bodies to know how unrealistic that was – but a skeleton with seaweed rather than hair clinging to her skull, and eye sockets with nothing in them. He shuddered. They should have stayed in the cottage, sitting in front of the fire with crumpets and tea. Perhaps it was a bad idea to have come down here to Cornwall in the first place.

Becca slipped her arm through his, as if sensing his unease. She tried to pull him close into herself, but he stood stiffly, like a man on guard, staring into the far distance. She kissed his cheek, whispered into his chilled ear, 'Let's go back.'

He frowned at her, then guided her down towards the sand, anxious she didn't slip, checking the steps for seaweed. And it was because he was so preoccupied with this that he didn't see Roxanne Lark until he turned his back on the pool and found himself face to face with her. He froze, and so did she. He felt Becca's hand tighten on his arm. He opened his mouth, but the only word that came out was a feeble 'Hello'.

Roxanne burst into tears, swung round and began to scurry across the beach.

'Hellfire!' a man said from somewhere above and behind Doug, and very loudly too. He pretended not to notice. Instead he took Becca's hand firmly in his and guided her across the sand towards the sea. The last thing he wanted was to look like he was following the woman.

'We could do with a few things from the shop,' Becca said. It was a simple enough observation-cum-request, but sometimes bad things start from very simple beginnings. 'There's a Sainsbury's at the top of town. You couldn't just pop up there in the car, could you?'

'I'll walk,' he said. 'I want to get to know the place. You never know what I might learn.'

So he walked down as far as the Brendon Arms, then swung right over the canal until he reached a small roundabout. From there he headed left along the edge of the shallow Neet estuary, before cutting right up the main street until he reached his destination.

It was just after he had selected a couple of 'ready-to-eat' avocados – he was sceptical of that description, so he selected them carefully – that he noticed a man watching him. He was tall and heavily built, grizzled hair, with a face that hadn't seen a razor for several days and a protruding right eye. For a moment Doug returned his gaze. The man puckered his lips and turned away. Doug shrugged and focused on what they needed, conscious that when he got home the chances were that Becca would be asleep on the sofa and it would be him who made their supper.

'You alright?' the woman overseeing the self-service tills said.

'I bought some wine. The machine thinks I'm underage.'

She laughed. 'Don't kid yourself, mate. You're fifty if you're a day.'

He laughed back, to show he could take a joke.

'Mind you, I like a bit of experience myself!' She winked. By Doug's reckoning, she was sixty plus herself.

'I'll keep that in mind.'

Doug made his way down the hill, a bag in each arm. It was only when he was nearly at the bottom that he spotted the bus stop. He hadn't noticed it coming the other way, but there it was, and he knew instantly it was the one where Josie had seen Layla and Raglan on that fateful evening: behind it was the shallow River Neet which flowed down to the beach. He had read all the press reports more than once, and this had to be it. He crossed over to it. There was no-one there. Layla and Raglan had been there about 7.30, at this time of year. He checked his watch – he liked wearing a watch even though a mobile phone rendered one irrelevant. It was just gone seven. Dark, but plenty of artificial light, so it would have been easy enough for Raglan to be recognised even from a distance. He hadn't denied it. He had freely admitted that he had been there and had given her a cigarette. So presumably he had spoken to her. Doug wondered what they had talked about.

He frowned. A bigger question was why was Layla at that bus stop in the first place? Taking shelter from the rain? *He ought to check the weather for that evening.* To meet someone? *If it wasn't Mick, then who else might it have been?* Or had she been waiting for a bus? And, if so, to where? *He ought to check out* the *timetables from back then if they were still available.*

His phone beeped. It was Becca, wondering if he was alright. She must be hungry. He messaged back and picked up his bags again and began walking, but not along the main road. Instead he walked a short distance along the river, pausing to admire a heron and wondering if it was the same one as he had seen from the Weir restaurant. He turned left over Nanny Moore's footbridge, which he had identified from his paper map. He loved his paper maps, a hangover of his days as a cub scout. Though quite who Nanny Moore was, he didn't have a clue. There was a sports club to the right, and tennis courts, but he could see no sign of activity. He pressed on. The sky was clear, moon and stars fully visible, and he paused, looking up. There was a plane heading west. Brits escaping to the warmer climes of Florida maybe. He felt a sudden pang that it wasn't him and Becca. Cornwall was beautiful, but at this time of year …

His musings were cut off by a man's voice booming out behind him. 'Oi, mate!' He hesitated, then carried on walking. 'Yeah, you mate. We want a word!'

Doug turned. There were three of them and they were closing fast. With a bag of shopping in each hand, Doug knew that breaking into a run wasn't an option. In any case, when it was a matter of *fight or flight*, he wasn't going to be bullied. He reckoned he was pretty good at talking himself out of situations, and, if not, he could handle himself. He wondered if the guy in the middle might be the man from the supermarket, but it was hard to be sure because he, like the others, was wearing a balaclava. To one side of him was another man, almost as tall, but much slighter, the slit of his face eerie in the half-light. The guy on the other side was squat, and he carried himself like someone who was always up for a fight. Doug tensed himself for whatever was to come and slowly lowered his bags to the ground.

'Is there a problem, guys?'

The man in the middle walked right up to him, so close that Doug could smell the beer and sweat. Doug decided that he was almost certainly the supermarket man. His mates positioned themselves slightly to each side, forming a distinctly threatening semicircle. Doug slipped his right hand into his pocket seeking a weapon, his car key or the cottage key, but he remembered even as he did so that they were both sitting in a blue glass bowl on the kitchen table.

'You're the problem, mate.' He spat the words out. 'You come down here causing trouble, upsetting people, working for that murderous bastard.'

'You mean Mick Raglan?'

'Course I bloody do.'

'He's dying of cancer.'

'Good job too.'

'Even though he is dying, he insists he is innocent.'

For a big man clearly past his prime, the guy moved fast, his right hand shooting out and grabbing Doug by the coat collar. 'I'm going to give you a choice.'

'Let go of me,' Doug said softly. He reckoned he could break the man's handhold, but he didn't want to exacerbate the situation. Talk him down. What was the saying? *A soft word turns away wrath.*

There was an explosion of pain in the left-hand side of his ribs. That was the squat man's right fist crashing into him, followed immediately by his left fist. So much for soft words. Another fist crashed into his ribs from the other side. Doug collapsed to the ground. He braced himself, waiting for the kicking that would surely follow, but nothing happened. He looked up, trying to take in what little bit of the faces he could see. Was that it? Was that the end of the warning?

'OK,' he said. He groaned and held up a defensive hand. 'Just leave me be. I've got the message.'

He started to clamber to his feet.

'Well here's a reminder in case you forget.' There was another punch, this time right in the middle of his face, and then another. Doug staggered, wiping at the blood that had erupted across his eyes, but he refused to go down. He stepped back, easing himself out of range. If they came at him again, he'd go for the tall guy. He was the weak link.

'Look out!' one of them hissed. 'We've got company.'

There was a couple walking towards them from the town. Doug could only just make them out, but the woman's boots were beating a tattoo on the tarmac. They stopped suddenly, the boots falling silent. No doubt the twosome were wondering what they were stumbling across. Then, without another word, the three men were off and running into the darkness, the squat one pausing to kick one of Doug's bags as he went. 'Enjoy your scrambled eggs, matey!'

By the time he had staggered back to the cottage, Doug's head was reeling. He banged on the door and almost collapsed on the floor when Becca pulled it open and gasped. 'What on earth?'

The advantage of living with a nurse with several years' experience of A & E is that a beating up by a bunch of thugs, far from throwing her into a panic, merely acts as a spur to action. She got him sitting down, made a phone call, ripped up his only white T-shirt and began to wipe him down.

'No shouting, Doug, no crying "It hurts". It's your own fault. You should have taken the car like I said. And I'm not wasting any of my clothes on you.' She wasn't wasting any sympathy on him either, it seemed. But Doug was glad just to be in her hands.

There was a banging on the door, and someone barged in. 'Here you are. My first aid box. And a few other things. Just use what you need. That's what it's for,' the woman said, all calm and efficient. Then her tone changed. 'Oh my God, what have they done to him?'

Doug opened his eyes and saw through the blood that the visitor was none other than Roxanne Lark.

'They beat the shit out of him,' Becca snapped.

'But shouldn't you take him to hospital?'

'And sit in a queue for hours? I'm a nurse, I've dealt with far worse than this.'

'Oh.' Roxanne sounded hurt. 'Well if you don't need me—'

'Sorry.' Becca was scrabbling through the box to see what Roxanne had brought. She looked up. 'I shouldn't have … look, I'm sorry. Why don't you make us all a mug of tea. I think we could do with it.' Then she returned to dealing with Doug.

CHAPTER THREE

THEY ATE BREAKFAST with a welcome watery sunshine angling through the window. Doug sat still while Becca bustled around and produced scrambled eggs ('it's amazing they survived' she joked) on brown toast, freshly brewed coffee, and orange juice. She kissed him on the top of his head, whispered 'you silly fool' and sat down opposite him. They began to eat.

'Can I just point out,' Becca said as she finished her plateful, 'that as strategies go for getting out of the chores, offering yourself as a punchbag to the local thugs wouldn't be one I would have opted for.'

Doug laughed, and immediately regretted it as pain somersaulted through his ribs.

'It'll hurt for a while, whether or not it's just heavy bruising or cracked ribs, but as for your face, that will never be as pretty again. So you're lucky I can live with a man who looks likes Quasimodo on a bad day.'

'I love you too,' he said. And he meant it absolutely.

He stretched out his right hand as far as he comfortably could, and she took it in hers. He saw tears in her eyes. She gripped his hand tightly. 'Don't do that to me again, Doug. I do want our baby to have a father.'

He would have said something back, something both heartfelt and soppy, but there was a rap on the door. Becca got up to answer it.

'Roxanne!'

'I hope I'm not interrupting, but I just wondered how the invalid was and if you needed anything. I'm going to the supermarket in a bit.'

'Thank you, but we'll be OK.'

Doug cut in. 'Come in and have a coffee.'

'I'm interfering. I'm sure you don't want me here.'

'I would still very much like to ask you a couple of questions.'

Roxanne hesitated. There was a look of alarm in her face. Getting them some groceries was on her agenda, answering awkward questions was almost certainly not.

'Look,' Becca said firmly, taking charge. 'This is how things are. I don't need to tell you that we are booked into this cottage for two weeks, so let me make it clear that we are not going to go home today or tomorrow or anytime early. Doug has a job to do, and he's going to do it. As you know, he wants to find out for definite who killed your daughter. The only thing you've got to make a decision on is this: are you going to help him or hinder him? You don't have to answer this minute, but you are most welcome to sit and have a coffee with us. Not here, but at the Olive Tree. Doug is not going to go into hiding. We will go over there and we'll sit out the front with a coffee, and we hope you will join us.'

'I'm not sure …' She was fumbling for the words, and her face was pale.

Becca pressed on. 'Would 10.30 suit you? Or perhaps this afternoon if that is better?'

'Yes, no, I mean 10.30 is fine. But … but … not out the front. Inside … if you don't mind.'

Becca released an enormous smile. 'Thank you. And thank you again for the medical stuff. I will replace everything we use.'

'Can I just ask one question myself. Are you planning to report the assault to the police?'

Becca turned towards Doug. He shook his head. 'I don't want to complicate things.'

Roxanne nodded. 'Thank you. I'll see you at 10.30.' Then she exited, closing the door quietly behind her.

Becca frowned. 'That was odd, wasn't it? Asking if you were going to report the assault?'

Doug drained the remains of his coffee. 'I expect she knows who they are.'

'You were pushing your luck with Roxanne,' Doug said. He and Becca were walking very steadily along the canal. This time it was she who was having to slow her pace for him.

'I had it under control.'

'You could have lost her, telling her we weren't going home early under any circumstances.'

'It's called woman's intuition, Doug. I knew exactly what I was doing.'

'Woman's intuition!' He grunted the words. 'That sounds sexist to me.'

'Trust me, Doug, we women know best.'

He stopped suddenly and gasped in pain. 'Hell!'

'You should have taken more painkillers,' she said. 'As I just told you, we women know best.'

'I'll make sure it's written on your gravestone.'

'On current form, you'll be dead long before I am.' She took his arm and gave it a gentle squeeze.

'Now come on, Doug, nice and steady, or the lovely Roxanne will get cold feet and do a runner.'

Roxanne hadn't done a runner. She was holed up at the back of the cafe, facing away from the other tables.

'I'll have hot chocolate with marshmallows,' she said without even looking up.

'I'll get them,' Becca said, leaving Doug to ease himself into a chair. He looked at Roxanne, but didn't speak. She looked back at him, but quickly dropped her eyes to her lap.

It was only after a considerable pause that Doug spoke, and when he did so, it was in a distinctly theatrical voice. 'Oh my God, what have they done to him?'

She looked up. 'What are you on about?' She shifted uneasily in her chair.

He sat upright, trying to stretch the pain out of his back, then fixed his eyes upon her. 'That is what you said to Becca when you came round last night and saw me.'

'Did I? So what?' She shrugged. 'Obviously I was concerned for you. It was a bit of a shock.'

'I can believe that you were concerned for me. But what is bothering me is what you said, or rather what you didn't say. You see, you didn't say "what on earth happened?" or "what has *he* done to him?", you said "what have *they* done to him?".'

Roxanne looked from Doug to Becca and then back to Doug. 'But … but when Becca rang last night, she said …'

'What I said,' Becca interrupted as she sat down next to Roxanne, 'was that Doug had been hurt and did you have a first aid box and anything to clean up the blood.' Roxanne half rose in her seat, but Becca stretched out her hand and took a firm grip of her arm. 'We really are on your side, Roxanne. We are on your daughter's side. So you have to trust us. Why don't you just sit down and do some breathing exercises for a moment, and when the hot chocolate arrives and when you are feeling calmer, we will continue.'

Roxanne subsided onto her chair and moments later began to sob silently. Becca produced a small pack of tissues out of her bag and passed it to her.

Doug watched, fascinated. He didn't get to see Becca 'in action' very often. He knew her well, of course, knew from personal experience that she was much more than just a competent A & E nurse, but he was impressed nevertheless.

'I'll share something with you, Roxanne,' she said softly. 'I had a child and she died too.'

Roxanne sat up sharply and stared across at her. 'You, you …'

She fell silent as a waitress arrived at the table with the hot drinks and cake. Silence remained after the girl withdrew.

'How?' Roxanne said eventually.

It was Becca who cried now. Roxanne passed a tissue back to her. Becca mopped her eyes and struggled to regain control. 'My beloved girl died as I was giving birth to her. After nine months of carrying her and loving her. I never saw her alive, never fed her from my breast, never, never …'

Roxanne stood up then. Doug thought she was going to leave, but instead she moved behind Becca and folded her arms around her shoulders and rested her head against Becca's. 'You poor girl.'

Doug sat still. He felt excluded from this pain. He felt unnecessary, an interloper to their grief, a man who had stumbled into a forbidden women's world. He had held Becca's child, grieved for it, and yet Alice had never been his. He felt like an imposter.

'Ask me your questions,' Roxanne said. She had returned to her seat, wiped her face again, and taken a sip of her hot chocolate which she held clasped between her hands. 'I can cry later.'

Doug cleared his throat. 'When you saw me last night and jumped to the conclusion that I had been attacked, and attacked by more than one person, was that because you were expecting me to be attacked? To scare me off?'

'No I wasn't. It's just that … that I wasn't surprised.'

'Do you know who they are?'

She shrugged.

'But if I were to describe them to you, you might be able to tell me who they were.'

'Maybe. But—'

'As I told you, I have no intention of reporting them to the police. I expect they just wanted to warn me off, and unfortunately they got carried away. Perhaps they wanted to protect you? Perhaps they didn't want to be confronted by the possibility that Mick Raglan wasn't the murderer, that there was a killer still free and living in the community here. Sooner or later I will bump into them and find out who they are. If I trawl the pubs tonight—'

'I'll help you,' she said quickly. 'Describe them as

best you can, and I will tell you if I think I know who they are. The only thing I won't do is speak to the police.'

'I'm coming with you,' she had said as they had prepared for bed.

'No you're not,' he had replied.

'Yes, I am.'

And Becca had won.

'I am your insurance. They aren't going to hurt you in front of me, and they aren't going to touch a pregnant woman.'

She was right, of course. She always was. They were safer together. But when she had said 'they aren't going to hurt you', it wasn't so much *they* as *he*. When Doug had described the big guy, Roxanne had identified him almost immediately. It was the bulging right eye that had been the clincher. Doug had noticed that when he had seen him in Sainsbury's and he was pretty sure that he had been the middle one of the trio.

'I'd say it was Frank Trent,' Roxanne had said. 'It fits and it doesn't come as a surprise to me. He's got a bit of a temper and …' She had paused at that point.

'And what? What's his connection to you or Layla or indeed to Mick Raglan?'

'His brother is Andy Trent, and Andy's daughter Naomi was one of Layla's best friends.'

'Right.'

'I guess we were in and out of each other's houses a fair bit, and Andy and his wife Judy were really good friends to me after … after Layla's death.'

Doug had left it at that. Better to ask his questions of Frank Trent directly. No need to press Roxanne, and no need to jump to conclusions.

Trent's house was an unprepossessing building on Kings Hill heading out of town, opposite a small business park. When Doug rang the bell it was answered by a petite woman, Chinese to look at. 'Who are you?' she said in an English tinged with the local accent. No fripperies or politenesses.

'Does Frank Trent live here?'

'When he's not out on his boat.'

'My name is Doug Mullen and I have an appointment to see him. This is my partner, Becca.'

'Come in.' She turned and led the way.

Inside there were two men. Doug recognised one of them immediately, the man from the supermarket with the bulging eye. 'I think you must be Frank Trent.'

'Yeah.'

'And I'm his brother, Andy,' the man in the wheelchair said.

The likeness between the two men was striking.

'Twins?'

'Yeah. But I'm the pretty one.' He pointed to his scar-free face. 'Peas in the pod when we were small, but time and tide and all that. Now your lady can sit down if she needs to, but we aren't offering a free cream tea or anything. Just ask your questions and then you can clear off.'

'It's your brother I have questions for.'

'And why would that be?' Andy said, apparently in charge.

'Because he and two mates of his beat me up two nights ago.'

'Two nights ago? Well I find that hard to believe because he was here all evening. We watched the football together. And then he went to bed, half pickled.'

'He must have a doppelgänger in town.'

'I'm his doppelgänger.' He folded his arms firmly in front of him. 'There aren't any others. So, now that we've sorted out this case of mistaken identity, you're most welcome to leave.'

'I need to go to the toilet,' Becca said.

'Come,' the woman said, and took her by the arm. She seemed uneasy, glad to get out of the room.

Doug waited until the door shut, and then moved a pace towards Frank. 'I have no intention of reporting your assault on me to the police. I certainly have no wish to expose your wife to having to lie on your behalf.'

'She's *my* wife,' Andy said sharply, so sharply indeed that Doug was taken aback. 'Her name is Judy. Born and brought up in Truro if you must know. The light of my life. Don't even think of making her speak to the police.'

'I've said I won't. I'm not interested in getting petty revenge on your brother. What I want to do is find out who really killed Layla Lark. Nothing more and nothing less.'

Andy laughed. 'Come on, everyone knows that it was Mick Raglan.'

'Maybe it was. But the odd thing is that he is dying, and yet he still denies it. If you look back through all the reports, he never did admit that he did it. It ruined his life, ruined his marriage and his relationship with his daughter.'

'If he's so bloody innocent, how come he's waited until now to make a fuss?'

'I think he gave up hope. And then his daughter got in touch after her mother Greta died. I expect you remember her?'

Andy glanced across at his brother, but neither of them said a word.

'It was only after that, when the daughter was going through all the paperwork and found newspaper articles about Layla's death and Mick's conviction that she discovered the truth about her father. She has finally started to visit Mick. And that is why he is now so determined to save her from the guilt and shame of having a murderer for a father.'

'You're giving me a cricked neck. Sit down.' Andy waved at a floral armchair. It had seen better days, and the springs were largely unsprung, but Doug's painkillers were wearing off and he was glad to rest.

'Frank, get us a beer will you. I'm sure Doug could drink one too.'

Once Frank had gone, Andy leant forward. 'Frank's a bit of a hothead. His heart's in the right place, but his brain doesn't always do him any favours. If he thumped you, I'm sorry. The fact is that he's a bit soft on Roxanne. Always has been, but she keeps him at arm's length. So I could understand it if he decided that the best way to protect her was to give you a warning. Stupid of course. Bringing attention onto himself. But that's Frank.'

There was a noise as first Becca and Judy appeared, and then Frank.

Frank put a mug of tea in front of Doug. 'Sorry, mate, but your missus says beer won't agree with your pills.'

Doug shrugged. 'Do you happen to know where any of the coppers on the case have got to? There was a Detective Inspector Danny Duke and a Detective Sergeant James Gooch.'

Frank laughed. 'Old Goochie is around still. Took early retirement, on health grounds supposedly, but more likely he spent too much time in the pub for the Chief Super's liking.'

'Duke killed himself,' Andy said, soberly. 'He was a good guy. They found him hanging in his garage about two years ago. I went to his funeral. It was packed out. May he rest in peace. To the Duke!' He raised his glass towards Frank, and the two of them drained their glasses in memory of the detective inspector.

'Where will I find Goochie?' Doug asked.

'At the Pirate, playing darts. It's his second home.'

Doug sipped his tea, conscious that his next question might not be so readily answered. 'If you don't mind me asking, I gather your daughter Naomi was a close friend of Layla. Would you be happy to give me her number or address?'

'Well, um …' Andy turned towards Judy as if he needed her approval. 'We don't want her bothered.'

Judy immediately interrupted. 'I've already told Becca.'

He swivelled to look at her. 'Why on earth—?'

'Because Naomi might remember something.'

'What on earth could she possibly remember?' For a few moments, there was a stand-off, he glaring at his wife and she staring back defiantly.

'Naomi and Layla were like this.' She gripped her hands together. 'That's why, husband.'

The Pirate was quiet. Not that Doug was surprised. It was barely 6.30 p.m.

'Is Goochie around?' he asked as the barmaid – white blouse, black slacks and a look of pure boredom on her face – poured him his half pint. Becca wouldn't approve, but he needed it.

'Soon enough,' she said without looking up.

'What does he drink?'

'Same as what you've got.'

'I'll buy him his first pint. You can put it on my card now.'

He went and sat in a secluded spot in the far corner of the room, a place from which he could enjoy some privacy whilst also observing anyone entering via the main door. Doug had studied the few contemporary photographs of DS Gooch, but when he arrived some fifteen minutes later, he didn't initially recognise him. The intervening years and a drinking habit had taken their toll. Round red face, a considerable stomach and all but completely bald. Despite that, as he approached Doug with his pint in his right hand, he was nervously brushing with his left hand the few grey hairs that he still sported.

He sat down heavily in the chair opposite and took a couple of gulps. 'So why have you bought me a pint?'

'I wanted to talk to you.'

'I guessed that. What about?'

'Layla Lark.'

'Ah! So you're the guy snooping around and upsetting people.'

'Snooping? Is that how you see it?'

'That case is history. We caught Mick Raglan and put him away and everyone was bloody grateful that we did.'

'He still denies he did it. Even though he's dying of cancer.'

Gooch laughed. 'Dying? That's the best news I've heard for ages. When it happens, there'll be one hell of a party down here.' He put his glass to his mouth and took another deep pull on his beer.

'What made you so sure he did it?'

'Because he was seen with her that night at the bus stop. Because she was a sexy little tart that probably teased him and then said "No". So he decided to teach her a lesson, but it all got out of hand.'

'So she was raped by him?'

'I can't remember all the details. It's a long time ago. Water under the bridge.' He stood up. 'Thanks for the drink, but that's all you're getting. I've got some darts to play.'

Doug thrust out his hand. 'Take my card. I'd like to talk some more another day. Maybe I can buy you lunch?'

Gooch took the card, glanced at it, and pushed it in his pocket. 'Maybe.' He downed the rest of his drink. 'Or there again, maybe not.' And he headed for the bar.

Doug stayed sitting, sipping at what remained of his beer. There were a trio of men with whom Gooch started chatting and while he kept an eye on them, he also scanned the pub for Frank Trent's fellow thugs, but no-one seemed to fit the bill. It was when the group of men moved off to take control of the dartboard that Doug got the opportunity he was waiting for. Gooch, as he was bound to do sooner or later, headed for the Gents, and Doug followed.

'You again,' Gooch said when Doug turned up at the next urinal to his own.

'Me again.'

'I hope you're not going to make a habit of drinking at my pub. This is for locals.'

'Tell me, DS Gooch, what is it you are not telling me? Andy Trent, Frank Trent, Josie Archer and now you. Why is it that you are all so glad to pin Layla's murder on Mick Raglan?'

Gooch glanced across at Doug so sharply that he scattered drops of urine down his trousers. 'Because he did it!' he snarled.

'Did he? Or is it that you *want* him to have done it.'

Gooch's face was a mask of fury. 'My advice to you, mate, is to leave things well alone.' Then he stormed out, still buttoning up his flies.

CHAPTER FOUR

DOUG WAS UP early. The ribs still hurt, and getting comfortable in bed had been a particular problem that night. He pulled on his clothes, skipping the shower and leaving Becca to sleep in. He wanted some gentle exercise, and a chance to clear his brain, and Rex, he was sure, would want to inspect the area and mark it in the way that all dogs do. He headed along the canal, and then up the path that led onto the cliffs. His target was a tall building up near the cliff edge, known as the Storm Tower. According to a tourist leaflet in the cottage, it had been built in the 1830s, but some fifty years later had had to be dismantled and rebuilt inland because of coastal erosion. The photo showed it to be an octagonal building with the points of the compass written on the outer walls. Inside there was sufficient space to protect a few people from inclement weather.

Doug walked steadily towards it. From time to time his ribs would complain at the work they were being subjected to, but he was something of a 'no pain, no gain' man, so he grinned and bore it as he had been taught to do by his mother and also by life. When he finally reached the tower, he was greeted by tape, and signs warning of the closeness of the tower to the cliff edge – though he could see that for himself – and the fact that it was going to be dismantled (again!) and moved away further from the cliff. He felt a pang of sadness for the old structure, but moved closer to the cliff so he could get a better view of the coastline and the cliffs below. *Don't push your luck anymore!* He could hear Becca's words of wisdom drifting in the winds around him, but dismissed them. There wasn't a single person in view on that part of the cliff top.

He got out the binoculars which she had given him as a birthday present, 8 x 42 magnification, lightweight and excellent quality. He hadn't used them in earnest yet, and this seemed the ideal place to try them out properly. He scanned the cliffs away to his left, and paused to admire a couple of black-headed gulls riding the winds which were blowing in from off the sea. Then he continued to traverse from left to right, across the sea, and north up the coast where the satellite dishes of GCHQ gleamed in the early morning sun. Then finally onto the sand of Summerleaze Beach, hovering for several seconds on the sea pool, and noting that he wasn't the only human up early with his dog.

His own dog, however, was uninterested in these other dogs or indeed any of the things that had caught Doug's attention. Instead his interest was engaged by something else. He was perched on the edge of the cliff, ears alert, and whimpering. Doug felt a frisson of panic that he had been so careless. He knelt down, grabbed the dog's harness, and clipped his leash onto it. Then Doug saw what the dog was looking at. Rex may not have been able to read warning notices, but there was nothing wrong with his eyesight.

'Hell!' He tightened his grip, looping the leash round his wrist. He knelt as far forward as he felt was safe, then lifted the binoculars again. There were two figures standing close to each other gesticulating, and in between them, lying on the rocks, was a body.

He swore and got to his feet. 'Quick,' he said to Rex, as if the dog had a perfect understanding of the English language. The two of them ran helter-skelter as fast as Doug could manage across the grass, keeping close to the cliff edge. All sense of playing it safe had evaporated. The dog was far too smart to fall down the cliff Doug told himself, and Doug was irrationally confident that he himself would avoid that fate too. Eventually he stopped. Rex turned and looked up at him. He had been enjoying the adventure. *What next?* his eager face said.

Doug grabbed the dog by the handle on the harness and began to scramble down the steep rock face. There was no time to weigh the risks. His ribs were howling their disapproval, but he ignored them. This was more important and his adrenalin was driving him on. By the time he reached the body, very clearly female – *could she possibly be alive?* – there were four onlookers, not two, and the two new ones were uniformed police.

'Is she alive?'

'Stand back please, sir. Medical assistance is coming.'

Doug ignored the advice. He took in the other salient details: white and red trainers, jeans, and a checked coat. And to judge from the blood on the woman's head and the twisted position of her body, and the fact that neither policeman had attempted to put the woman in the recovery position, he knew without any doubt that she was dead.

'Sir, would you move away!' One of the uniforms was standing right in front of him. 'It's probably a suicide or accident, but just in case it isn't, we need to minimise contamination of the scene.'

'I doubt very much that it's either of those,' Doug said firmly.

'Just move along please, sir. We will be taking a list of names, just in case we need to contact you, but in the meantime I must insist you move well away from the body. And do keep your mutt under control.'

'Do you know who she is?' Doug asked.

'Just move along. How many times do I have to tell you?' The copper was young, and clearly struggling to cope. 'Please,' he pleaded.

'Will do. But I think you'll find the dead woman is Josie Archer.'

'You know her?'

'I met her a couple of days ago. She was pretty distressed then. Anyway, here's my card. I'm staying in Bude for a couple of weeks, in case anyone wants to speak to me.' And with that he held out a tired-looking business card, while telling himself at the same time that he really did need to get some new ones professionally designed and printed. The officer took it and looked at it in bemusement. Then he stared at Doug as if trying to work out if he was a bit of a head case. Nevertheless he had the presence of mind to pass the card back to Doug. 'Write your holiday address on the back, if you don't mind, sir.'

Doug didn't mind, and he did just that.

Doug got the call from the police that he had been

expecting, but it was several hours later. Just ten minutes after that there was a knock on the door, but within those ten minutes, he had a short, sharp argument with Becca.

'What on earth were you doing, saying that? You might as well have sent them a written invitation to come and arrest you?'

'Calm down. They aren't going to arrest me.'

'Serve you right if they did. Anyway they're bound to tell you to pack your bags and clear off back to Oxford.'

'They can't make me.'

'Really, Doug, what was the point of you showing off about the woman's identity? I thought your idea was to keep a low profile while you tried to find out what had really happened to Layla.'

'Ever since we realised Roxanne was Layla's mother, and I told her why I had come to Bude, our cover was blown. She must have talked to people. Hence the three amigos who came and beat me up. So as far as the police are concerned, it's better to come clean now than get found out later.'

'You were even stupid enough to tell them you've only met her once, and you handed over a card announcing that you're a private investigator.'

'I don't want them to assume that it was an accident.'

'She may have committed suicide.'

'Maybe she did. I don't know. But I want the police to know the whole picture and to investigate it properly. Not just assume Josie tripped and fell.'

Becca shook her head, and then swore, though this wasn't aimed at him. She placed both hands, fingers outstretched, onto her stomach and grimaced. 'This is going to be hell. I'll be enormous by the time I get to nine months. Give me a hand with these boots.'

'Aren't you staying?'

'No. You can deal with them on your own. Sort out your own mess.' Doug got down on his knees. It was first time she had asked for this sort of help. He slipped her purple Doc Martens on her feet, and laced them up carefully. She stood up, pulled her coat on and slung her bag over her shoulder.

'Thank you,' she said suddenly, before kissing him on the cheek. 'One bit of advice. Turn the recorder on your phone on. Of course, don't tell them you're doing it. Just remember, they are going to be very suspicious of you.' And with that she left the cottage.

When the two detectives arrived less than five minutes later, Doug studied their ID cards carefully, trying to memorise their names. He had made up a fresh cafetière, but they both refused his offer of a coffee. He guessed this was their way of demonstrating their professionalism. DI Kate Jennings was dressed in a subdued green jumper, slim-fit black jeans, short brown boots and a bright green waterproof coat which she peeled off and hung on a peg by the door. She had short ginger hair, pale green stud earrings, and eyes that roamed the room, assessing Doug and his environment. By contrast, DS Chris Bristow was morose and messy, in dark blue trousers, shirt and jacket, none of which matched or fitted his ungainly frame. His skin was weathered and, like his silver-grey hair, betrayed the fact that he was long past his prime.

'You are Mr Doug Mullen?' Jennings said.

'Yes.'

'And how is it you are down here in Cornwall out of season?'

'My partner and I were offered this cottage for a couple of weeks. It's nice to have a change of scene, even out of season.'

'According to your business card you are a private detective.'

Doug nodded. He was in no mood to proffer unsolicited information. Besides he was curious to see exactly what questions they would ask.

'You told one of my colleagues that you believed the dead woman was a Josie Archer.' She let the unspoken question tail off.

'Wasn't I right?'

'Was she a friend of yours?'

'I met her two days ago. She was wearing a checked coat and trainers when I met her, and she had long blonde hair. So when I saw the body from up on the cliffs – my binoculars are very powerful – I jumped to what turned out to be the correct conclusion.'

'Would you like to tell me what that meeting entailed?'

Doug sighed. He couldn't face messing about being evasive. If she didn't already know, Jennings would soon pick up all the gossip that was doubtless circulating the town. 'I am investigating the death of Layla Lark. You will probably be aware that Mick Raglan was found guilty of Layla's murder some fifteen years ago. It was all over the news. His daughter's mother died a year or so ago. Mick himself is still in custody, but he is also dying of cancer. He asked me to clear his name. He insists that he was innocent, and he wants his daughter to be able to live the rest of her life without that terrible sense of guilt that she is the daughter of a murderer. Anyway, it was his daughter who actually hired the cottage for us.'

'So what did you and Ms Archer discuss?'

'I bought her a cream tea and I asked her various questions about Layla, but she was very reluctant to answer them. As you may know, Layla and Josie were very good friends, along with their fellow schoolmate Naomi Trent.'

'I do know. When I was training, one of our lecturers had a particular interest in the case.' Jennings smiled. 'Mr Mullen, Doug, I wonder if I could change my mind and have a coffee, with nothing added. Sergeant Bristow is a milk and three sugars man. And where's your toilet?'

Quite apart from needing to pee and fancying a coffee, it soon became apparent that Jennings had several more questions up her sleeve.

'So when you saw Josie Archer close up, what was going through your head? I understand you came scrambling down the cliffs in considerable haste.'

'I'm not sure what you mean. I was hoping she wasn't dead, but of course it was obvious that she was. To judge from the injuries, I assumed at first that she had fallen from the cliffs. But because I had spoken to her less than forty-eight hours previously and she had been very resistant to my questions about Layla Lark, I decided it was unlikely to have been an accident. That seemed like too much of a coincidence. You see, it was Josie Archer who saw

Layla and Mick Raglan together at the bus stop on the night of Layla's murder. But maybe that was not all she saw that night. Maybe she knew something else that would have undermined Raglan's conviction.'

'And maybe,' DS Bristow butted in, 'you had so alarmed her by your aggressive questioning, that she did indeed just decide to kill herself.'

Jennings glanced at Bristow, but there was no reprimand for him from Jennings. Instead she was fully focused on Doug's face and waiting for him to reply.

'I was not aggressive in my questioning.' Doug spoke with exaggerated slowness. Inside his head he was spitting feathers, but knew he had to maintain control. If he exploded in anger, then that would support the possibility that he was an aggressive questioner. 'I met Josie in a public place. We had a cream tea together. If you go and check with the staff at the Weir, I don't think you'll find anyone to support your baseless speculation.'

Doug was hoping that Jennings might call off her attack dog, but she continued to observe what was going on like a bookie watching a dog fight, with cool fascination. Bristow sneered. 'OK, we'll leave speculation till later, but here are the facts. Fifteen years after the death of Layla, you turn up on a mission to prove Mick Raglan innocent. You track down and interview the woman who as a child testified to seeing Layla and Mick together shortly before Layla was brutally murdered. Less than forty-eight hours later, Josie ends up dead. I agree it is unlikely this was a coincidental accident. I would maintain that it is much more likely she was so traumatised by the questions you asked her that she jumped off that cliff to avoid any more.'

'Or, of course, the third possibility is that someone pushed Josie off that cliff in order to stop her saying anything else to me, or indeed to you police.' Doug was not going to be cowed. 'But let's suppose that your suicide theory is correct, Sergeant. What it underlines is that Josie very likely did know something more about Layla's death, and also knew that whoever it was who murdered Layla, it was not Mick Raglan.'

'I think we have covered the possibilities very adequately,' Jennings said, bringing the two growling dogs under control. 'We will await the results of an autopsy and any forensics before we can draw any conclusions on the manner and events surrounding Josie's death. But to move on, Mr Mullen, I do need to ask you where you were last night.'

'I was here most of the time, except for between about 6.30 and 7.30 or a bit later. I was in the Pirate pub for about an hour. One of your former officers, Detective Sergeant Gooch, will be able to confirm that.'

She smiled. 'Gooch in the Pirate. Now there's a surprise.'

'I bought him a pint, but he wasn't very friendly.'

'So you've been catching up with Jim Gooch as well as Josie Archer. You have been busy since you arrived here.' She stood up. 'Very nice coffee,' she said, making it sound like she had just experienced the most marvellous of social events. 'Is there anything else I need to know before I go off and do some investigating?'

'I was attacked the other evening.'

'Oh!' Whatever answer she might or might not have been expecting, the alarm-tone of her voice indicated this particular one was not one of them. She sat down again. 'I assumed you'd had an accident.'

'Three men did their best to beat the living daylights out of me.'

'Any witnesses?'

'A couple at the end, but both they and my attackers beat a hasty retreat at that point. But if you think I am making it up …' He pulled up his shirt to reveal some impressive purple and black bruising.

'And did you report this?'

'No.'

'Of course you didn't,' she sighed. 'And would you mind me asking if think you might be able to identify the persons involved?'

'They were swathed in balaclavas, hats and scarves.'

'So you've no idea at all?'

'I certainly have some ideas, in fact I am pretty sure about one of them.'

'Would you like to give me a name?'

'No.'

'Any particular reason why not? I should add that I am not in favour of personal vendettas being conducted on my patch.'

'Because I am not certain. And just for the record, I am not out for personal revenge. I am merely trying to get to the bottom of who killed Layla Lark.'

'That sounds to me like the business of the police.'

'But it isn't, is it? It hasn't been the police's business for the last fifteen years.'

'We don't continue to investigate cases that have been done and dusted.'

'Indeed you don't. Which is why Mick Raglan and his daughter approached me for help.'

Jennings pulled on her coat, a clear sign that she had had enough. Doug had had enough too, but was pretty pleased at how it had all gone.

'Any time you need a coffee …' He smiled.

Jennings didn't smile back. Instead she handed him a card. 'That's just in case you change your mind and have a burning desire to be more cooperative in the future. Or perhaps you prefer to be a lone voice crying in the wilderness?'

With that, she and DS Bristow made their exit. And seconds later Becca made her entrance.

She sniffed, smelling the coffee and noting the mugs on the table. 'Did you remember to record it?'

'I decided not to.'

'No surprise there, then,' she said as she pulled her coat off and sat down opposite him. 'Anyway how did it go? At least they haven't arrested you.'

After he had told her in some detail and she had listened in silence with pursed lips – not necessarily a good sign – she placed her hands palm down on the table and gave him her Paddington Bear hard stare. 'When I was a child,' she said, 'I found a wasp nest in the garden. Being a curious little girl, I poked a stick in the hole to see what would happen. Well, what happened was a swarm flew out like a horde of avenging angels and I ended up yelling and screaming all the way to the house.'

Doug nodded.

'Do you see any parallels?'

He shrugged.

'I sometimes wonder why on earth I fell in love with you, you idiot.'

* * *

Mick Raglan is Guilty as Charged
Layla's murderer was a Sexual Predator

The nightmare is over for the people of Bude. Residents of the Cornish holiday town are today breathing a deep sigh of relief after 'evil' sexual predator Mick Raglan was found guilty of the murder of fifteen-year-old Layla Lark, a pretty blonde schoolgirl found floating face down in the iconic sea pool on the town's Summerleaze Beach.

After a four-week trial, the jury pronounced a unanimous guilty verdict. Whoops of relief and tears of grief erupted from the visitors' gallery. An emotionless Raglan was led away, with the words of the judge ringing in his ears. Justice Knight announced that he would hand down a sentence the following Monday, but he warned Raglan that he should 'expect no mercy for a heinous crime'.

Outside the court, Layla's mother, Roxanne, was too distraught to make a public statement. Her solicitor, Madeleine Osborne, stated that they were expecting the harshest sentence possible. 'There are no mitigating circumstances. My client will wake up every morning of her life knowing that her daughter is dead, murdered by a man with no conscience and no mercy. No mercy should be shown to him. He brutally murdered Layla, leaving her to be found in the sea pool by people looking forward to an early morning swim. May he rot in hell, and may Layla be forever comforted by the angels.'

Candice Kipling, Crime Reporter

'What are you doing?' Becca said as she padded into the kitchen, still in her nightie, dressing gown and slippers.

Isn't it ruddy well obvious? Doug was feeling irritable, having been awake since shortly after 5 a.m., but he was wise enough not to express his thoughts out loud. The clue to what he had been doing was the state of the kitchen table, which was large enough to comfortably accommodate the six persons who normally stayed in this cottage, not to mention a couple of guests. But right now the surface was covered with cuttings from the national and local newspapers. He had laid them out in the order in which they had been published, and had been reading through them again from beginning to end in search of inspiration. Zoe Finch had provided them all. When she had arrived at the only meeting that she and he had had, she had plonked on the table two box files jam-packed with all the press coverage of the case.

'I hired someone to assemble this for me. I can't bear to read it. What my father did … what he is alleged to have done … but I guess this will give you a start.'

'Do you believe your father is innocent?' Doug had said, and immediately regretted it.

But she had merely shrugged. 'No,' she said. 'But he wants you to investigate the girl's death, so what does it matter what I think.'

'I merely wondered …'

I don't care what you wondered,' she snapped. 'I am paying you a lot of money, so the least you can do is earn it.'

Doug could remember Zoe's words as if it had only been yesterday. And it was those words which stuck in his head, and which had, intermittently, been circulating inside his brain ever since. 'I am paying you a lot of money.' Not 'he is' or even 'we are', but 'I am'. Even though the money was, as far as he had understood, Mick Raglan's. Even though she thought her father was guilty. Even though she would presumably get it when he died. 'I am paying'. *For him. Because I desperately want him to be innocent, even though I know in my heart of hearts that he's guilty.* Was that what she had meant?

Back in the present, Doug stood up from his chair and gave Becca a desultory kiss. 'These are all the news reports from the case.'

'What time did you get up?'

'I couldn't sleep, so I thought I'd lay everything out and go through it all again methodically.'

'And has that been helpful?'

He frowned. 'Not much.'

'So why don't you go and give yourself a nice soapy shower and put some clean clothes on, and after that you can make us both some scrambled eggs for breakfast. In the meantime, I'll take a look through all this stuff and see if I can make sense of it. As my aunt Aggie used to say, there is a lot to be said for a second pair of eyes. And that is especially true if the eyes belong to someone who doesn't look like a walking zombie. Hell, Doug, you're even kissing like a zombie this morning.' She grabbed him and kissed him long and hard on the lips. 'That's how you do it.'

'I might just check the internet first,' he said, 'in case there's anything about Josie on it.'

Doug stared at the computer screen in disbelief. How long does it take for news to spread round a place like Bude? Or indeed round the whole of the internet world?

It was barely 7.30 a.m., and a single search had brought a brand new article to his attention. 'Death in Bude – "Murder!" he said', the headline screamed.

Doug read on, cursing under his breath as he did so.

An Accident, Suicide or Murder?

Early this morning, the body of 32-year-old Bude resident Josie Archer was found sprawled on the rocks on the southern side of the Summerleaze Beach. An unfortunate accident? That was the immediate assumption of the medics and police who attended the scene. But one Doug Mullen, a private detective allegedly 'on holiday', thinks otherwise.

Mullen is in fact working for Mick Raglan, who 15 years ago was convicted of the death of 15-year-old Layla Lark. Lark's body was found early one morning floating in Bude's iconic sea pool.

Mullen is being paid by Raglan to find any evidence that might get the original conviction quashed. Mullen spoke to Josie Archer two days prior to her death. It is very likely that the conviction of Raglan was high on his agenda because 15 years ago Josie Archer was the key witness in the case. It was she who saw Layla Lark talking to Raglan at the Strand bus stop on the very night of the murder.

So was Josie's death an accident? Was she driven to suicide by Mullen's aggressive questioning? Or did someone push her off the cliff to shut her up.

Be assured that I will be keeping you informed as this story unfolds.

Check the links below this article for more details on this extraordinary case.

Candice Kipling, Crime Reporter

'Breakfast in five minutes. I thought you were going to have shower, Doug.'
   'Look what they are saying.'

'Who are saying?'

'You read it.' He stood up and walked over to the front window, peering out to see what the weather was like. It was wet and windy. He tried to focus on the branches being blown around, and the clouds careering across the sky, in the hope that this might dissipate the anger and sense of betrayal he was feeling. He had tried to be honest, he had tried to lay out the complication of the facts as he saw them, and within hours his name was being blazoned across the press. He had wanted to stir the police into action and maybe get them on his side, but not this.

'You're being paid to find *any ... any* evidence that might get Raglan's conviction quashed!' Becca's indignation levels were rising fast too.

'It makes me sound like a money-grabbing shit for hire.'

'Driven to suicide by Mullen's aggressive questions. Who the hell does this woman think she is?'

'That's what Sergeant Bristow accused me of yesterday. Aggressive questioning.'

Becca stood up, her face transformed with fury. 'So they've leaked the contents of your interview to a journalist.'

'One of them must have. I know that Kipling reported on the original case. I've read her reports. But all the stuff about Josie, well that's got to have come from the police. Still you did warn me. Poking sticks in wasp nests and all that.'

'And look where it has got us, Doug! This sort of sensationalist reporting will make you a target for more reprisals.'

'Sensationalist reporting sells papers and advertising space on the internet. This sort of thing is perfect click-bait material.'

'Don't be so calm, Doug. Plug yourself back into the real world. Every day we stay here, Bude is getting more and more dangerous. You've been attacked. Josie is dead, and one way or another everyone is going to blame you. Are you just going to carry on as normal?'

'Not as normal. But taking reasonable care.' Doug spoke with exaggerated calm. This had become a familiar routine in their relationship – her emoting for all she was worth and him being so laid back that at times he was almost horizontal.

'OK,' she said, now speaking in measured tones. 'Might I ask what, in practice, exactly does "taking reasonable care" mean?'

He sidestepped her question. 'Right now, I'm going to ring DI Jennings.'

'Ah, your new buddy inspector! So I assume that means you will be asking her what the heck is going on?'

'Yes.'

'Good, because if you don't, I will.'

Jennings looked at her phone, saw 'Doug Mullen' on the display, and killed the call. It was not as if she wasn't expecting it. It was only early, but thanks to the powers of the internet, the report by Candice Kipling had already sent ripples – actually, not ripples, but wild white-horse waves – right across the local police network. Jennings was still shivering from an ice-cold video call with the Chief Super, who had asked what in Hades' name was going on and did she feel she was in control of things, or did she need some 'support'.

Of course she asked for some more uniforms on the ground to calm the people of Bude and speed up house-to-house enquiries, although she was well aware that for him the word 'support' had meant someone more senior to take charge. The story had only been alive a few hours, so to expect her to have solved the mystery of the death already was totally unreasonable.

She made her way out of the temporary base they had set up in an empty shop unit, and took shelter round the back from the weather and prying eyes. She got out her mobile and returned Doug's call. Better now than have him ring again at an awkward moment.

'Hi, Doug?' she said, her voice full of false cheer. 'How can I help you?'

'I've just been reading Candice Kipling's article.'

'So have I, Doug. It's very unfortunate. I imagine you must be feeling rather cross with her. Actually I'm not too happy because it has already provoked a very tricky conversation with my chief superintendent.'

'I don't care about your superintendent!' The voice had changed. It was a woman and she was taking no prisoners. 'Was it you or was it your two-bit sergeant who leaked the contents of Doug's discussion with you yesterday?'

'I don't know what you mean?'

'"Was Josie Archer driven to suicide by Mullen's aggressive questioning?" That's what that wretched

Kipling wrote, and "aggressive questioning" are precisely the words which your side-kick sergeant used when he was trying to make out that Doug drove Josie to commit suicide.'

'I don't remember it being quite like that.'

'Doug recorded your interview on his phone. We don't have to remember what it was like. We just have to replay the recording back.'

Jennings tried to say something in reply, but she could find no words.

'If Doug ends up being attacked again, you will be finding yourselves in hot shit, so I strongly suggest you find out who leaked this, and make sure that that person is despatched to a Siberian gulag for an extended period.'

The line went dead. If the woman had been ringing from an old fashioned phone, there would no doubt have been the noise of the receiver being slammed into its cradle. Who was she anyway? Mullen's partner or wife, she guessed, unless she was a pet gorgon who he kept in his bedroom to deal with wretched police detectives. Jennings sighed. How she would like a phone to slam down sometimes, to get her frustration out of her system. Or indeed a pet gorgon. Jamila was a wonderful wife and mother, but a gorgon she was not. As it was, she couldn't rely on anyone else to rescue the situation by apologising and appealing to Mullen's sense of reason. That was for her to do. But with Mullen's gorgon standing guard over him, there was no point in doing an immediate ring back. Best to leave it for half an hour. In the meantime, she needed to have it out with Chris bloody Bristow.

She marched back into the shop-cum-office channelling her inner Tina Turner. Bristow was there as were DCs Liam Protheroe and Rhona Fernie. Lying on the floor trying to do something with computer cables was Chas, all long hair, lousy complexion and (most surprising of all) an obsession with the Beatles. He was singing 'Let It Be' loudly and tunelessly.

'Right,' she snarled, 'which of you bastards has been talking to the press?' She had decided it was best not to focus on Bristow despite him being the obvious suspect, although when she had finished scanning the room it was inevitable that her gaze came to rest on him.

It was one of those pin-drop moments. Chas had not only stopped wailing, but had stopped moving too and was looking up at her with his mouth half open. Protheroe and Fernie were both studying the floor as if they had never seen another one like it. As for Bristow, he looked guilty.

'Chris,' she smiled. 'Do you remember using the words "aggressive questioning" yesterday? During our conversation with Mr Mullen.'

'I'm … I'm not sure.'

'OK. So let's try another question. Did you speak to – or in any other way communicate with – Candice Kipling?'

'No.'

'OK, question number three, did you have a conversation with anyone else yesterday evening, a conversation in which any details of the case might have inadvertently slipped out?'

There was a long pause, the sort of pause during

which every incidental sound – from Chas's asthmatic breathing to Protheroe's nervous scratching of his shaven head – was magnified.

'I … I … I bumped into Jim Gooch and … well he asked how it was going and …'

Another prolonged pause, this time without ancillary noises. More a collective holding-of-breath hiatus.

'If you have any further communication with that man during the course of this investigation, then you have my promise that I will personally castrate you.'

There was what sounded like a snigger from Chas. She glared down at him and then round the room. 'Nothing that I have said now and nothing regarding the case is to be discussed with family, friends or even pet guinea pigs. As for your penance, Sergeant, I have yet to decide what that will be. But in the meantime you can have the pleasure of going out in the rain and getting each of us a nice hot drink and pastry. Mine is a flat white with an extra shot.'

'Of course, ma'am.'

'And, just for the record, I am treating the death of Josie Archer as a potential murder case until such time as it is clear that it isn't.'

Becca and Doug ate their scrambled eggs on toast in silence. The toast was somewhat burnt and the eggs were rather dry, but he barely noticed. His brain was spinning like a toy he had had as a child. One of his mother's male friends have given it to him to curry favour with her. It was red and chrome. You set it on this stand, and gave it a twist, and once it had started spinning, it whirled round and round and round for

71

ages, almost frictionless. He had kept a tally of how long he could get it to spin before it finally toppled off its perch.

'A penny for your thoughts, Doug?'

He looked up at her and frowned, as if he couldn't understand who she was or what she was doing there, this woman licking her fork with infinite care.

'Come in please, Doug, your time is up.'

'Sorry, I was … I was …'

'Miles away.'

He sat up straight and eased his chair back. 'You told Jennings that I had recorded the meeting.'

She smiled. 'I did.'

'She'll be worried.'

'That's the idea. Actually, no. The idea is that she takes this case with the utmost seriousness, and she starts by sorting out who the leak is in her office.'

'I trust her.'

'In that case, you're a fool. You don't know her well enough to do that.'

'Even so—'

'Actually, the truth is that I recorded the meeting.'

Doug looked at her in amazement. 'You what?'

'I left my phone on the dresser, the recorder app turned on. Probably just as well I did. You never know if we might need to produce it as evidence.'

'Evidence?'

'Evidence that your interview with the police became public property within hours. Evidence that we are not going to be pushovers.'

Doug stood up, took his mug and both of their plates over to sink, where he rinsed them before slipping them into the dishwasher. 'Thank you for the breakfast,' he said, and trudged off upstairs for his belated shower.

Three quarters of an hour later, they were both cleansed and dressed, and Becca was struggling to put on her boots. 'Time to get back on the horse, Doug.' He looked up from the computer, on which he had been searching for anything new on Josie. He had also, though he was never going to admit it as such to Becca, been obsessively reading the many comments that Kipling's piece on Josie has been garnering.

'What horse?'

'When you've fallen off a horse, the key thing is to get back on it again before you lose confidence in yourself. So we should get ourselves out there in Bude and see what happens.'

He nodded. 'I just need to finish what I'm doing here. It won't take long.'

'OK. I'll head off to the Costa in the main street, and I'll wait for you there. Don't be long.'

'Want a hand with the boots?'

'Please.'

When Doug set off, he had no particular plan in mind beyond meeting up with Becca. 'If you have no expectations,' Becca had said just before she left, 'then you can't be disappointed.'

Doug had grunted an acknowledgment. What with that and the 'get back on the horse' comment, she was full of words of wisdom this miserable morning. But actually, on this occasion, events were about to demonstrate the wisdom of her truisms.

As he was walking along, head down against the drizzle, he didn't see – or rather didn't recognise – Roxanne Lark because her back was turned towards him. She was standing still, talking to someone, and he had almost passed her before he heard a screech, and a hand grabbed his sleeve. 'Oi, you!'

The woman with her was much younger, late twenties maybe, and her skin was almond coloured, and her hair straight and black.

'This is him,' Roxanne said.

The woman looked at Doug. Her face, like that of Roxanne's, was anything but friendly, but she said nothing.

Roxanne wagged her index finger at Doug. 'If you hadn't come here, Josie would still be alive,' she hissed.

Doug didn't need anyone to tell him that. For the last twenty-four hours, ever since he had seen Josie Archer's body on the rocks and realised that she was without any doubt dead, guilt had enveloped him. If he hadn't started asking questions in Bude, if he hadn't agreed to investigate on Raglan's behalf, if he hadn't tracked her down and asked her questions …

'Well, haven't you anything to say for yourself?' Roxanne was spitting with fury. 'You spoke to her didn't you! I've read the report on the internet. It'll be in the local rag, too, I dare say. You bullied her with your questions, and so she went and climbed up on the cliffs and jumped.'

'I didn't bully her. I asked her a few questions over a cream tea. That was all.'

'Oh, buying her a cream tea makes it all right, does it?'

'I don't believe she jumped. I don't believe she stumbled and slipped either. I think she was pushed, that is to say murdered.'

'What on earth makes you think that?'

He tried to use reason. 'I cannot prove it. Nor can the police. But I believe that someone arranged to meet her up there on the cliffs, and when she arrived I believe they pushed her over the edge to her death. She was a key witness over your daughter's death. Maybe there were other things she knew but never said. The likelihood is that the same person killed both Layla and Josie, and if that is the case then Mick Raglan cannot have killed your daughter.'

Roxanne was breathing heavily. 'Even a shit like Raglan has friends. He lures you down here to Bude, he arranges for some mate to kill Josie shortly after you have spoken to her, and people jump to the conclusion that the deaths are connected. Then before you know it, the media and the do-gooders will be flooding into the town and screaming "Miscarriage of justice" and "Let Raglan out".'

'That seems unlikely,' Doug said.

'Why? Why is it unlikely? He's a devious bastard and he's had plenty of time to come up with the plan.'

'I can see you are upset.'

'She's not the only one.' The other woman stepped forward and prodded him in the chest. 'Suppose it's me next?'

Doug studied her, and realisation dawned. 'Are you Naomi Trent?'

'Too right I am. Me and Layla and Josie were best friends back then. Inseparable.'

Doug was silent. How could he truthfully reassure her that she had nothing to fear, that whoever killed Josie wouldn't try and do the same to her?

'Well?' she demanded. 'Who is going to keep me safe? Because let me tell you, if you're right, if there's a killer prowling round Bude, then I'm scared as hell that the killer is going to come after me next.'

'Do you live alone?'

'I do, now that Josie is dead.'

'I see.' Mullen looked at her. She was small like her mother, and her Chinese traits were obvious. Rather vulnerable too. 'Maybe I can help?'

'You? What are you talking about?'

Before he could answer, his mobile rang. It was Becca, wondering where he had got to. 'I've just bumped into someone,' he replied. 'Can you order me a cappuccino? And just a moment.' He turned to Naomi. 'Can I buy you a coffee or something? Then we can talk about keeping you safe.'

Naomi looked at Roxanne, but Roxanne merely shrugged. 'Got to go.' And she stalked off.

Doug stood rooted to the spot, watching Roxanne walk away. And walking away was what it felt like. She might have supported him in all of this. What was going on inside her head? The road she was taking led to the beach. He watched her pass the fateful bus stop, where Layla had been smoking with Mick Raglan on that last night of her life, but she didn't even glance at it. Instead she strode on face forward, looking neither right nor left, shutting out the memories and the pain.

'Honestly,' Mullen said, turning back to Naomi, 'I think we should talk.'

'Doug, are you still there?' Becca's voice broke in on the mobile.

'Wait,' he replied.

Naomi was staring at him. 'Is that your wife?'

'Partner.'

Doug waited. He could see that she was torn, and he couldn't think that he could say anything else to persuade her.

'I'll have a hot chocolate,' she said suddenly. 'And a sticky bun, because I never got round to breakfast.'

'OK.' It felt like a small step forward.

'But just to say, I'll never feel safe again. And that's all down to you.'

The problem with even small steps forward is that they can be followed by big steps backwards. They were two-thirds of the way up the hill when a man intervened. He must have spotted Naomi and taken umbrage at her walking side by side with Doug because he jay-walked across the road, ignoring the horn of an irate driver, and came to a stop right in front of them.

'What's going on?' He glared at her as if he had a divine right to know everything about Naomi's life.

'This is Doug.'

'Boyfriend? You don't half get through them.'

'Not a boyfriend,' Doug said quickly. 'And who are you?'

'Her brother. Half-brother to be precise. I like to keep an eye out for her.'

'You're Joshua.'

'Mr Trent to you.'

'Have you lost your balaclava?'

'You what?'

Doug was pleased to see that he was taken off guard by this. He pressed on. 'The black one you were wearing three nights ago when you punched me in the ribs.'

Joshua licked his lips and ran the back of his hand along them. 'I dunno what you're talking about.'

'What's going on, Josh?' Naomi was looking at her brother. Either she had no idea about the attack or she was a top class actor.

'I was assaulted by three men,' Doug said, turning to face her. 'One was your uncle Frank. It seems that another was your brother. I dare say that in due course I'll find out who the third one is. He's tall and skinny, but hasn't got a very good punch. Unlike Joshua.'

'I don't know what you're talking about,' he blustered. 'Let's go, Naomi.'

'No,' she replied. 'Doug is buying me a hot chocolate.'

'I said, let's go.'

'So what can you tell us?'

DI Jennings had addressed the question to pathologist Ros Price. The 'us' was herself and DS Chris Bristow. What was it someone once said? Keep your friends close and your enemies closer. She didn't particularly see her sergeant as an enemy, but he was certainly someone she needed to keep a beady eye on. Only time would tell if he had learned his lesson or was actually a deep-dyed treacherous bastard.

'Well, Kate, it's an interesting case.' Price paused for a moment. She was not the first pathologist that Jennings had encountered who had a taste for the theatrical.

'In what way?' Jennings was happy enough to play along with her, anything to keep her cooperative.

'Obviously there is no doubt in my mind that the poor woman did fall from a very great height. The trauma injuries are totally consistent with that. Of course, the question in your mind will be what caused her to fall from this very great height. Did she just slip? Maybe. Did she jump? Impossible to rule that out, I think. Or was she pushed by some person or persons. Again, I can offer a firm maybe on that too.'

'Any sign of a struggle prior to her fall? Any sign of bruising that might indicate that?'

'Hard to tell. Hard to distinguish any such injury from the injuries caused by the fall. Of course, we will do a thorough forensics sweep of the body and clothes in case that sheds any light, but getting to a firm conclusion on this one will be tricky. Otherwise that's about it, until and unless forensics come up with any further information.'

Back in the car heading for Bude, Jennings was pensive and silent, so much so that Bristow decided to strike up a conversation. 'A penny for your thoughts, ma'am.'

She turned and frowned at him, then sighed.

'No thoughts, except that if it was murder, I hope there was no struggle. Just a simple quick push that was totally unexpected by her. Maybe Bill Franks will be able to shed some light on it.

They parked near the Tourist Information and headed off on foot in search of Franks. He was, as he had said he would be, up on the cliffs above the bay. Franks was the scene of crime manager, and he was standing next to a stretch of the cliff that he had cordoned off with the usual tape. A couple of other white-suited colleagues were packing up stuff. The rain up here was more unforgiving that it has been down in town, but Jennings barely noticed.

'Was she on her own, do you think, Bill?'

'Two different sets of footprints.' He pointed to where there was some scuffing of the ground. 'That looks like where she fell from. We'll need to do proper analysis, but to my eye one set of prints look very much as though they match hers. As for the second set, they are larger, so arguably might be a male's.'

'So we're looking at murder.'

'I didn't say that, so don't say I did.' He was glaring at Bristow who was trying to makes notes on his damp notebook. 'It looks very much as though she had someone with her. In which case it could be murder, but if she and some bloke were having a lovers' tiff, then who is to say that it wasn't just an accident, that it got a bit heated, she slipped, he tried to grab and save her – I am sure a defence lawyer would be able to come up with a very convincing scenario along those lines.'

'So murder or an accident, but not suicide.'

'I never said that, either. But suicide is, typically, a solitary business.'

Jennings moved away, up to the end of the tape, and moved as close as she dared to the edge. She stared down. There was a taped-off area down there too where Josie had died. As she took it all in, Jennings realised that it would not necessarily have been an entirely instantaneous death. A struggle on the grass, the terror rising in the poor woman as it became clear to her what was going to happen. After that, a plummeting fall which would surely have involved colliding with and bouncing off outcrops of the cliff, before the final free-fall descent onto the rocky floor below. Jennings suddenly felt decidedly queasy.

'Are you alright, ma'am?' Bristow said, interrupting her musings. 'With respect, you are rather close to the edge.'

His words seemed ethereal and distant. She looked down and nothing seemed real. She felt herself rocking gently, backwards and forwards. What was going on? Then someone shouted, and she felt a hand grab her tight by the arm and pull her back. She collapsed to the floor, and when she looked up she saw Bristow and Franks peering down at her.

'I thought you were going to fall, ma'am,' Bristow said. He seemed genuinely alarmed. 'You, you—'

'You were far too close to the edge,' Franks said. 'We don't want any more bodies on our hands.'

'Sorry. I don't know what came over me.' She eased herself onto her knees and then up onto her feet. She brushed herself down and then made a pronouncement. 'Whoever the killer is, he must be a ruthless bastard. Imagine pushing someone and watching her bounce all the way down to her death. And after that walking calmly away and resuming your normal life.'

'Best not to dwell on the detail, Inspector,' Bristow said. 'Best to focus on catching the killer.'

'I'm sure you're right.' She paused and turned to her sergeant. 'In that case, let's go and do just that.'

They had nearly reached the car when Jennings told Bristow to go and get himself something to eat. 'I think I'd better see if Mullen is at home and try and pour oil on troubled waters.'

'In that case, don't light a fag while you're doing it.'

'A fag? I don't smoke.'

'That was a joke, ma'am. I do know you're a clean-living woman who has the good sense not to pollute her lungs. It's just that that was what my old gran used to say, before she passed away, bless her.'

'Sorry. I'm not sure I'm quite myself today.'

'We're making progress, aren't we?' Bristow seemed to need reassurance. He was working hard to recover the ground he had lost with his boss.

She nodded. She felt they were.

'Would you like me to come along and keep you company. I could apologise in person and—'

'No, Chris. But thanks.'

When she got there, the door opened before she was able to press the bell. A woman glared at her. 'You must be DI Jennings. Doug said you had texted.'

'Might I come in? I feel I owe the both of you an apology.'

'He's not back yet,' she said, standing firmly on the threshold of the door. 'Gone shopping. And maybe snooping too. I'm Becca, by the way. What do I call you?'

'I am happy to be called Kate.'

'Well, Kate, do you have actual news that I can pass on to him?'

'As a gesture of goodwill, I wanted to tell you and him that after talking to both the pathologist and crime scene manager, I have decided that it is most likely that we are looking at a case of murder. I cannot prove that, of course, but I am conducting the police investigation on that basis.'

'Good.'

'I have also discovered the person who leaked information to the journalist and am confident that it won't happen again.'

Becca nodded. 'I'll let him know.'

'Please keep this information strictly between yourselves. I hope to make a statement to the Press either today or tomorrow, but I have to clear it with my chief superintendent first.'

Becca smiled. 'No leaks from this house, I can guarantee that.'

'Thank you. Just one more thing. I don't think we have your mobile number. Best if we do. Just for the record.'

Becca shrugged and scribbled it down on the back of an sales leaflet. 'Worried I'll do a runner?' she said as she handed it over.

Jennings turned to go, but Becca called her back.

'Kate.'

'Yes.'

'I was a bit over the top. No hard feelings?'

'It wasn't the best start to my day.'

'Nor ours either.'

* * *

Naomi turned left off Kings Hill and down onto the footpath which led across the Bude marshes and nature reserve to the canal and from there to the beach. There was an early morning mist, which gave her a sudden pang of regret. That was something she would really miss.

How many times had she and Layla walked that route, escaping from the restrictions of home, stopping to admire the men doing their rugby training and showing off their physiques, not to mention huddling down on the bank of the River Neet to share a cigarette or two, sheltered by a clump of bushes from all but the most observant of passers-by.

'I can't wait to get out of here,' Layla had said on more than one occasion. Naomi hadn't taken her that seriously. Everyone she had known at school had complained about Bude, but when push came to shove, Bude was what most of them settled for. And that was what she had settled for.

Now she wished she was a thousand miles away. Anywhere but here. She paused to see if the heron was standing sentry down on the river, but she could see no sign of it. She pushed on. She had made her decision, there was no turning back. That would be failure. Joshua's behaviour yesterday had been the final straw, treating her as if she was still a schoolgirl and using his strength to impose his view. Enough was enough.

When she got to the front door, she didn't hesitate. She felt she owed Mullen an explanation. She wasn't going to go into any details, but she needed to tell him her plans, so he wouldn't worry. She pressed the bell twice and drew a deep breath. Through the frosted glass window of the door, she saw the outline of someone approaching.

'Hello? Can I help you?' The woman standing in front of her was wearing a purple dressing gown and was holding a wooden spoon in her hand.

'Is … is Mr Mullen in?'

The woman scowled. She clearly didn't take kindly to being interrupted this early. 'And you are?'

'Naomi.'

'Ah.' Her name seemed like a magic word. *Open sesame*. 'You'd better come in then. He's in the shower.'

'I'm really sorry. Perhaps I should come back later. Perhaps I shouldn't have come at all. It's stupid of me. I hadn't thought that you might not be up and …' She dribbled to a halt. And then she began to cry.

'Are you going somewhere?' he said.

Naomi looked up and realised that Doug was looking at the bulging rucksack which lay at her feet. They had all eaten breakfast. Becca had given Doug's portion of scrambled egg to Naomi, leaving him to eat muesli. He had seemed rather quiet, almost depressed, and occasionally he felt his ribs.

'I need to get away,' she said. 'I don't feel safe.'

'Do you have somewhere to go?' Becca asked. 'Somewhere to stay?'

'Not really. I have a contact in London, I'll sleep on her sofa until I can find digs and a job.'

'Are you scared that you'll be the next person to be found dead at the bottom of the cliff?' Naomi gulped. Becca had asked this this as if it was the most normal question in the world. 'And do you think someone pushed her?'

'I don't think Josie would have jumped. She wasn't like that and, besides, she didn't like heights.'

'Perhaps she had an attack of vertigo and just fell?'

She shook her head. Why would Josie have gone and stood on the cliffs? It made no sense.

'Doug and I think she was pushed, murdered by the same person who killed Layla.'

Naomi put her head in her hands and began to rock. It was like a nightmare, a never-ending nightmare. How could this have happened to Josie? She had seemed rather on edge, but nothing more than that.

'We don't think it is safe for you to stay on your own in the flat you shared with Josie. We've discussed it and so we'd like you to stay here.'

Naomi opened her mouth, but no sound came out, largely because she had no idea what to say. Had she even heard Becca correctly? She could stay with them?

'This is a big house. You can stay here with us for as long as we are here. Then, if you still want to leave, you can come with us to Oxford. It will be safer than London.' Becca seemed nice. She had a really genuine smile. And her being pregnant made her seem particularly reliable, someone she could trust.

'Really?'

'Yes. Really. We will keep you safe.'

'But you're pregnant. Won't I be in the way?'

'Being pregnant makes me a very protective person, and rather dangerous when I or anyone I care about is threatened. Ask Doug.'

Doug cleared his throat. 'I feel responsible. So actually I would be very concerned if you didn't stay. Also, I think you might be able to help me out.'

'You mean you want to ask me a load of questions.'

'I imagine you knew Layla and Josie better than nearly anyone else.'

'I suppose so.'

'So if you think you might want to try staying with us for a day or two, that would be fine by us. And if at any stage you change your mind, well that is fine too. Becca will show you your room. And when you're ready – and really only when you are ready – I hope we might be able to start chatting.'

'Tell me about Layla.'

Naomi frowned, as if this was a surprise question. 'Well, we were mates.'

'You mean you and Layla. What about Josie?'

'Well her too of course.'

'What did you get up to?'

She shrugged. 'What do you think? We were teenagers.'

'Smoking behind the bike shed?'

'Not literally. But sometimes we'd have one down by the river on the way home.'

'Your parents wouldn't have approved?'

'No. My dad smoked, but he made it clear we weren't to.'

'So Layla bought them?'

'Yeah. Or blagged them off people.'

'What about boyfriends?'

'What about them?'

'Did you have one? Or was it a case of sweet fifteen and never been kissed?'

This provoked a laugh. 'What girl hasn't been kissed by the time they're fifteen? Not that my first kiss was anything to get excited about.'

'Sex?'

'No.' She said this very quickly. 'My mum and dad would have killed me if I'd got pregnant.'

'What about Layla?'

She thought about this for several seconds before answering. 'I don't think so. I mean, she never told me she had, you know, "done it". I can't be sure.'

'But to judge from what I have read and heard, and from the photos, Layla was very attractive. I imagine she must have had a boyfriend.'

'No-one very serious. She was pretty. Could twist the boys round her finger when she wanted to. She was a bit of a tease.'

'But was there anyone in particular hanging around Layla at the time of her death?'

'I don't know.'

'But you were one of her best friends?'

'I tell you, I don't know.' For the first time, Doug caught a glimpse of Naomi's agitation. And, also he sensed for the first time that she might not be being entirely truthful. He knew for a fact that Layla had not been a virgin when she died. That had been established by the autopsy. There were no obvious signs that she had been subjected to rape just before she had been murdered. Did that mean she had had a lover or had it been a one-night stand? She had presumably been attracting attention from males, whether at school or outside. But was that from Mick or someone else? In any case, why was Naomi so cagey about it now, years later?

He decided to change tack. 'Tell me about Mick Raglan.'

It was clear that Naomi was taken unawares by this question, because her mouth opened and closed like a fish that had just jumped out of the sea and mistakenly landed on the deck of a boat.

'What sort of guy was he?' Doug pressed. 'Did you see much of him?'

'Not a lot,' she said, answering only the second question.

'But you knew him?'

'He sometimes did deliveries for my mum's home cooked meals business. Often holidaymakers didn't want the bother of collecting their meals, so she would cook them and she'd get Mick to deliver them.'

'Why Mick?'

She frowned. 'Dunno. He lived in the next road so that was convenient. During the day he was a decorator and odd-job man. There was plenty of work out of season doing up holiday cottages. But during the season, that was different. So I guess working for my mum in season and picking up a bit of extra money would have been very helpful.'

'If he lived nearby, you must have bumped into him often enough.'

'Occasionally. He'd hoot at us from his van sometimes. But why would I have been interested in him?'

'I was wondering if maybe he was interested in you.'

Naomi began to breathe heavily. Her face flushed. 'Are you asking me if I had sex with him?'

'I suppose I am.'

'No I blooming well didn't. I was only fifteen.'

'Maybe he was more interested in Layla or Josie.' Doug tossed this out as a casual observation. To judge from the photographs he had seen, Layla must have been the most obviously attractive of the three teenagers, and Naomi maybe the one who would have attracted the least male attention. Could some jealousy and sexual rivalry have developed between the two of them?

Naomi said nothing. Doug wondered if perhaps he was treading on dangerously sensitive ground. He didn't want to lose her cooperation or even put her off from staying with them – God forbid that she fled and then ended up dead.

'Sorry,' he said in a sudden rush. 'I've asked too many questions. Please don't take it the wrong way. It's just that I can't get a handle what sort of man Mick was.'

Naomi took a deep breath and sat up straighter. 'At the time, it never occurred to me. But actually, I have sometimes thought that he was more interested in my mum than any of us girls.'

'Really?' Mullen was genuinely surprised. 'And yet, according to one of the news reports I have been reading, he sometimes gave Layla lifts home.'

'Only once, as far as I am aware. I met up with her outside school one day, and she said she wasn't feeling well, so I rang Mick and he was working in Bude, so he popped round and drove her home.'

'Did you go with them?'

'No. Layla lived at the other end of Stratton, so it would have been out of my way. I just walked home as usual.'

Doug hesitated before his next question, uncertain as he was about how Naomi would react. But now that it had popped into his head, he knew he had to ask it. 'May I ask how it was that you had Mick's number stored on your phone?'

If he hoped Naomi might be taken off guard by this question, he was out of luck. She replied without any hesitation. 'Because I helped Mum with her business. Often it was me who rang Mick up to line him up for a delivery.'

Doug was about to ask another question, but Naomi's phone rang. She answered it, then stood up and went outside.

'Maybe give her a break?' Becca said. She had been sitting in an armchair, unusually quiet.

'If she wants to.'

'Doug.' Her tone of voice was one that he recognised all too well, especially when it was followed by a stilted silence. 'You don't want to press her too hard.'

Doug nodded, as if he agreed, but actually that was exactly what he wanted to do. Press her until the truth came out, whatever it was.

Naomi came back inside. 'It's Kay, from the hairdresser. She's short-handed and has asked me to come in. I really need to be earning money as long as I am here.'

'What time would you finish?' Doug said.

'Five.'

'It will be getting a bit dark by then. I'll come along and be waiting for you.'

'You mean so you can walk me back here? Like I was a primary school kid?'

'I will be very discreet. You may not even notice me. Just walk back here. If anyone is watching or following you, I want to see who they are. If you want my protection, then you need to cooperate.'

'Alright. I guess you're in charge.' She held her hands up in a gesture of surrender. 'Sir.'

'One more thing. I don't want to scare you, but if anyone rings you or wants you to meet them, just remember it is possible that they might be the person who killed Josie. So text me the name immediately. OK?'

'Blimey.' She stared at him. The reality of the situation was beginning to hit home. 'OK.'

'I could do with a haircut,' Becca said, breaking her silence. 'Why don't I walk round there with you and see if they can squeeze me in?'

'You might have a wasted walk,' Naomi said. 'I would ring if I was you.'

'No, I need a bit of fresh air.'

As soon as Naomi disappeared back upstairs, Doug asked Becca what was going on. 'I need some fresh air?' he mimicked.

'We promised to keep her safe. Anyway, she was telling me earlier that her bitch of a boss won't give her enough work, so I thought I would go in with her and see if I could persuade the woman to reconsider the way she treats her staff.'

'How on earth are you going to do that?'

Becca had smiled her naughty smile. 'Now that, Doug, would be telling.'

Doug smiled back and kissed her. He had long since learned not to underestimate her.

'Anyway, don't I deserve a nice haircut?'

'Is that you, Zoe?'

'Yes.'

'This is Doug. Doug Mullen.'

'Oh.'

'I have a favour to ask.'

Doug waited for an answer, but there was none.

'Zoe, can you hear me alright?'

'You're going to ask me to visit my father, aren't you?'

'I need you to ask him a question for me.'

'The answer is no.'

'I really, really, really need you to say "Yes".'

Becca took an almost immediate dislike to Kay. She was as sweet as pie to herself and to the other customers, but towards her staff she was anything but.

It started almost as soon as they got in there. There was a jibe about Naomi's timekeeping. 'I had to stop off en route at the toilets near the tourist information,' Becca said, 'and Naomi kindly waited for me.' But this cut no ice with Kay, who had then insisted on doing Becca's hair herself, as if Naomi couldn't be trusted with a new customer. When she treated the work-experience girl with undisguised disdain, Becca decided she had had enough. She waited until she was paying, and then went into full attack mode.

'I hope you'll come again,' Kay said, inadvertently giving Becca the perfect opening.

'Unlikely,' she replied.

'Oh!' Kay was clearly taken aback.

'You see I'm here on business. Undercover, you might call it. I am currently working for an organisation which is interested in staff working conditions. And I have to say I have not been impressed. Criticising staff in front of customers. Taking on an intern who hasn't been allowed to even pick up a pair of scissors so far today.'

'I don't want her ruining a customer's hair!'

'But she's meant to be here to learn. You are meant to be teaching her, aren't you? And Naomi was telling me how erratic her hours were. Never knowing whether she would be able to pay her bills at the end of the week.'

Kay had turned pale. Becca could see that her criticisms, however fair or unfair they were, had hit home.

'Of course,' Becca continued, 'as an organisation we are interested in improving conditions for the worker, not in naming and shaming employers. That would be a last resort. So there will be a colleague of mine visiting in the next few weeks to see if things have improved. In the meantime, my advice to you would be to get your act together sharpish.'

And with that she turned and left.

'You might as well go home, love,' Kay said.

Naomi looked at her phone. It was 4.30.

'I don't mind hanging around until five. I could do a bit of clearing up, or something.'

Outside the light was failing, and so too was her self-confidence. Doug wouldn't be here until maybe a few minutes before five. Suppose someone was outside waiting for her? What if she was followed?

'No need,' Kay said. 'I'm going to lock up early. I want to get home. No point in hanging about.'

Naomi got her coat and swung her bag over her shoulder. 'How about tomorrow?' she asked in hope rather than expectation. She knew she wasn't anywhere near the top of Kay's list. That was what came of speaking out about the pay rates in front of the customers.

'Yes, I could do with you tomorrow. Nine-thirty, but make sure you're not late.'

'Thank you. That's very kind of you.' Naomi despised herself for being pathetically polite, behaving as though Kay had done her a massive favour. Clearly Becca's words had had an effect, but how long would that last? 'Have a good evening, Kay,' she added. *Squirm, squirm, squirm*. But she needed the money, and, until she had decided what her plans were, she would do whatever she needed to do in order to keep in her boss's good books.

Outside it was cold. A sharp northerly wind sweeping down the street. Above her head the clouds were bowling along. She resisted the temptation to look around and started walking down the hill. It was only a ten-minute walk. She would probably get to the house just as Doug was leaving. Anyway, who was going to follow her? The light was fading fast, but it wasn't dark as such.

She walked steadily, her senses on high alert. And very soon her senses told her that there was someone behind her, and to judge from the sound of their feet, they were moving faster than her, and so getting closer. She tried to increase her pace, without making it obvious. *Keep calm. Nothing can happen to you, not when there are other people around.*

'Oi, Naomi, hang on there.'

She recognised the voice, but kept on walking. The footsteps accelerated, breaking into a jog.

'I said wait!' Naomi stopped and turned. She couldn't outrun him. Probably it would turn out to be nothing. 'What's up, Matt?'

He grinned. It was a lopsided grin, and one which did nothing to make her feel comfortable. *Creepy!* That was how the three of them had always thought of Matt Tomkin. Mr *Creepy!*

'Where are you off to? You don't live down this way.'

'Mind your own business, Matt.'

'Hey, no need to get snarky, darling.'

'I'm not your darling, never have been and never will be.'

'How about an ice cream?'

'You must be joking. It's freezing.'

'A hot chocolate then? My treat. I've come into a bit of money, so I thought I'd share a bit of my luck with you. How does that sound?' He unleashed his unnerving grin again.

'Another time, Matt.' She tried to sound firm and friendly. You had to with Matt.

'Me not good enough for you?' he hissed, and stepped closer to her.

She felt fear then, remembering the warnings that Doug had given her. Why hadn't she texted him?

'I need to get home,' she whimpered.

'But you're going in the wrong direction for home. Or are you taking the scenic route over the marsh? 'Cause it's getting a bit dark. But I'll tell you what, I'll escort you shall I. In fact, you can slip your arm through mine, just like they do in the old films. That way you'll feel really safe.'

'OK,' she said. 'You can keep me company, but no need for the arms, Matt. Is that a deal?'

She knew the importance of maintaining boundaries. She had done some volunteering for the food-bank, and they had given her half a day's training on keeping oneself safe.

'Deal,' he replied, albeit reluctantly.

She had handled the situation well, she told herself. The last thing she wanted was for him to know where she was staying now. Anyway, he wouldn't hurt her, and Doug would surely be leaving the house any minute now. If she walked very slowly, if she could just delay things, he would find her and rescue her.

The problem with trying to slow him down was that he had such long legs that he naturally went fast and was soon turning round to chivvy her along.

'Come on, slowcoach.'

'Alright.' She had no option but to walk a bit faster. Initially they were walking close to the canal, but before long the path curved left. She tried to think of how to escape him or resist him if he made a grab for her, but she had nothing on her that she could use as a weapon. She had read a book in which a woman used a biro to stab her attacker in the eye, but she doubted she had one in her handbag. And surely it wouldn't be necessary.

They walked on until he suddenly stopped. 'Come on.'

She heard a sound then, behind her, someone running, someone who wasn't very fit. She could hear him wheezing and soon enough he went past. He – it definitely looked like a man – was wearing a dark tracksuit with the hood pulled over his head and trainers with a white stripe. By now she herself had caught up with Matt. In front, maybe fifteen metres away, the runner let out a groan and bent down, hands on knees. He glanced back at them, but beyond that showed no interest. He was panting and moaning as if he was about to have a heart attack.

'Now, princess, don't do anything silly, but we need to have a little chat.' Matt was so close to her that he could have grabbed her with ease. As for the man bent double, she had another, terrible thought, that he was part of it, that he was keeping watch and that if she tried to escape by running towards him, far from helping her, he would stop her. She glanced across at him again to see what he was doing and thought she saw him look back at her, and then back down at his feet. She realised with alarm that even if she shouted for help, he was too scared to intervene. Fight or flight was the saying. That guy was clearly a flight man.

'What do you want to chat about, Matt?' She tried to sound calm, but her voice wobbled.

'You know what I wanna talk about.'

'Let's talk as we walk,' she said. *Placate him, put him off his guard, be nice to him.* The words came to her from somewhere. 'Matt, I'm meeting a friend in ten minutes.'

'Liar! Do you think I'm a fool?'

She tried to think of something to calm him down, but she couldn't. No *fight or flight* for her. Just *freeze.*

His arm snaked out and grabbed her arm. 'No shouting,' he hissed. 'Just pretend we're a couple taking a nice romantic walk.' He bent his head over hers and sniffed at her hair. 'You smell really nice.'

She shuddered. 'Stop it, Matt.'

'Now, why don't you be a good girl and tell me what you told him.'

'Told who?'

His fingers dug into her arm. 'Don't play the little Miss Innocent with me. The guys want to know.'

'Everything alright?' The words came from behind them. They both turned. It was the wheezing jogger.

'Piss off,' Matt snarled. 'We're having a bit of private time.'

'Let go of her, arsehole,' the jogger said. He spoke softly, but not so softly that Matt couldn't hear him.

Matt let go of Naomi's arm and turned to fully face the man. 'What did you call me?'

'He called you "arsehole",' Naomi said.

Matt's attention flashed back to her. 'Shut it, bitch!'

If he hadn't said that, maybe Doug would have behaved differently, but those three words were like a spark dropped into a barrel of gunpowder. One moment he was under control and working to a precise plan, and the next he exploded. His first punch, a right-hander, smashed into the guy's gut, and then the second, a left-hander, jabbed into his ribs. Matt howled with pain and doubled over. As he straightened up to retaliate, Doug grabbed him by his coat with both hands, and then rammed his knee up into his groin. He howled again and collapsed onto the ground, where he lay moaning feebly.

Doug stood over him. His blood was up. He wanted to do more damage, to exact further revenge for his own beating and to make sure that the guy didn't hassle Naomi ever again.

'Got the message? Leave her alone!' Doug was breathing heavily, his ribs ding-donging with pain after the sudden exertion. 'Or shall I give you a final reminder?'

'No,' Naomi squealed.

Doug turned. There were tears in her eyes. 'Leave him,' she gasped. 'That's enough.'

Doug's fury evaporated. A moment ago the guy had been terrorising her, and now she was pleading for him. He nodded agreement, then scrabbled in his pocket until he found a tissue which he passed to her. 'Sorry, it's a bit crumpled …'

She spun away from him and walked off back down the path. He followed her, keeping a distance, unsure of how he now stood with her. He had saved her, and yet she was angry with him. He felt bad. A deep sense of shame engulfed him. This wasn't how he liked to think of himself. He had been poised to kick the guy's head in, in an act just as thuggish as what had happened to himself the other evening. Not so much an eye for an eye, as a kick in the head for a boot in the ribs.

As they approached the canal, Naomi slowed to a stop, allowing him to catch up.

'Sorry,' he said. 'I lost it for a moment. It's just that—'

'I don't like violence,' she said firmly, almost prissily, like a schoolmarm of yesteryear.

Sometimes violence is the only option, he thought, but he didn't have the balls to say it to her. 'I'm glad to hear it,' he said instead, aware of how lame it must sound.

'But …' She hesitated. He waited. 'But if I had had a biro in my pocket, who knows what I might have tried to do to him. Maybe tried to stick it in his eye.'

'When we get back,' he said, 'you might like to talk to Becca about it. She's better than me at those sort of things.'

'Don't do yourself down,' she replied.

Somewhere to their left, over the marsh, an owl hooted twice. They walked on steadily, in an almost companionable silence.

CHAPTER FIVE

THE TABLE WAS laid for breakfast. That is to say, there were three places – bowls, side plates, mugs and cutlery – closely packed up one end of the long table. The rest of it was still taken up by all the press reports and the like. But Doug's interest was, temporarily at least, not on any of these.

After the excitement of the previous evening, he had had his best sleep so far in the Cornish sea air. When he woke up, he dressed quickly and took Rex for a walk along the canal and onto the beach. And it was while the dog was scampering around vainly disturbing the sea birds on the sand that he found the name of DI Danny Duke drifting around in his head, and once Duke had surfaced, he refused to go away. Doug felt an overwhelming need to find out more about the man's death. Ever since his own army friend Ben had killed himself, Doug had found himself becoming almost obsessed with suicide. What drove people to do it? Why? Why? Why?

Duke had died less than two years previously. He had been in charge of the investigation into Layla's murder. He had been head of the team which saw Raglan convicted and put away for life. Raglan insisted he was innocent. Was there a connection?

He turned round and headed back towards the canal, calling to Rex as he did so, and to his surprise the dog came charging after him. Perhaps he could sense the urgency in his master.

Back home, he ignored all the piles of paper – and the dog's breakfast. Instead he went and logged on to his tablet computer. Then he started to search. It wasn't hard to find the relevant articles, the initial reports on Duke's suicide, the coroner's report into his death, and a short piece on his funeral, but it was another piece which most caught his attention. This was a personal interview with DS James Gooch. He read it through, and then read it through again.

The Worst day of a Detective's Life

It is part and parcel of being a police officer that sometimes they encounter very unpleasant events. But for DS James Gooch – known to his friends and colleagues as Goochie – the worst was not the aftermath of a terrible car accident or a drugs-related gang shooting but something altogether more traumatic.

Five weeks ago he drove to Camelford to pick up his senior officer, DI Danny Duke. 'I gave a hoot when I arrived, but by the time I'd had a quick fag, he still hadn't appeared. So I went and banged on the door. I didn't use the bell because he was getting a bit deaf, and besides I was already running a bit late, which was why it seemed so odd that he wasn't ready for me. I had half expected him to be standing there on his doorstep, and then tapping on his watch as I pulled up. I knew his wife was away visiting her elderly mother.

Maybe he had overslept. So I rang his mobile. He didn't answer it, but I could hear it ringing from inside the garage. The garage door was down, but I remembered he had a door on the side of the garage so I went and tried it. It was locked, but there was a glass window on the upper part, so I peered in.'

Goochie fell silent at this point when he related the story to me. It was clearly too painful, and yet he was determined to tell me. Eventually he cleared his throat and continued. 'I saw him almost immediately. Or rather I saw his feet and legs, swinging very slightly in a draught. I thought I was going to vomit, but my concern was for him. I put my shoulder to the door and smashed it open. I'd told him more than once it was too flimsy, and warned him that one day some young thugs would break in and steal his tools. Of course, once I got inside, it was obvious he was dead. I felt just above his ankle. There was some warmth left in the body, so he hadn't been dead for that long, but dead he most certainly was. I rang for support and went and sat outside on the doorstep and smoked maybe three or four cigarettes until the cavalry arrived. It was the worst day of my life.'

Candice Kipling, Crime Reporter

Doug paced around the room, stared out of the window at the canal and then sat down again. He sent an email and leaned back in his chair. Upstairs there were giggles of glee from the two girls. Maybe it was disrespectful to think of the pair of them as 'girls' but from where he sat they sounded like a pair of schoolgirls gossiping about boys in the year above them or the clothes they were going to buy and the club they were going to gate crash despite being under age. He smiled. He only had himself to blame. He had asked Becca to make Naomi feel at home – 'maybe she will speak more freely if she feels she can trust us' – and she was certainly doing that.

They almost bounced down the stairs, cheery as larks. 'We need some porridge, love,' Becca announced, as if they were in a hotel and Doug was the put-upon waiter.

'Of course, madam.'

'And coffee and orange juice,' she continued as she slumped down onto one of the chairs

'Yes, madam.'

Naomi was slightly discomforted by this exchange. 'Perhaps I can help.'

'No need,' Becca said cheerily. 'Doug likes to think he's a modern man.'

'Thank you, Naomi,' he said quickly, thinking things might be getting a little bit out of control. 'But it is kind of you to offer.'

The combination of porridge, juice and coffee seemed to calm Becca down, and after they had finished he showed them the article on Duke's death. Naomi and Becca sat side by side and read it in silence, except for the occasional intake of breath.

'Do you remember Duke, Naomi?' Becca said with exaggerated casualness.

'Well, yes, but …'

'I expect he interviewed you at the time, you being a close friend of Layla?' Becca hadn't forgotten that keeping Naomi safe and close at hand opened up opportunities to ask questions and, most importantly, get answers.

'Actually it was Goochie, DS Gooch, who asked the questions. There was some constable with him, but he didn't say a word.

'And what did Gooch ask? Can you remember. I know it's a long time ago, so it's probably a daft question.'

'He wanted to know if I had seen Layla that day. Of course, I had seen her, because we were in the same class for a couple of subjects. Often she'd be hanging around waiting for me and Josie at the end of school, but not that day. After that, I never saw her again.'

'Was that unusual?'

Naomi thought about it for a moment. 'Not really. She was her own person.'

'Maybe she was meeting up with a boyfriend. After all she was a good looking girl.'

'None of them lasted,' Naomi said.

'And why do you think that was?'

Naomi stood up. 'I need to go to the toilet.'

'She knows something,' Doug whispered, as if afraid that she might overhear them.

'I'm going to lay off the questions,' Becca replied firmly. 'Or she'll take fright. If you go out for the day, maybe I can make progress.'

That was when his mobile rang. It was an unknown number, but he answered it nevertheless, half expecting it to be someone trying to sell him a mobile phone upgrade. He had had enough of them in recent weeks. His name was probably on a list entitled *Hopelessly old mobiles. A soft touch with the right sales pitch*. Instead it was a woman announcing herself in strident tones as Candice Kipling.

'Thank you so much for ringing me so promptly,' Doug gushed.

'So you say in your email that you're a private detective investigating afresh Layla Lark's tragic demise. What makes you think I could help you? I'm just an old has-been of a journalist.'

'Even if you are – and I doubt it – can we meet and I'll explain?'

'Two conditions.' She spoke in brisk, heavily modulated tones. 'One: you buy me lunch in Camelford. Two: if you are successful in your quest to prove Raglan innocent, I get your "How I did it" story. Agreed?'

'Agreed, but I have one condition too.'

'I hardly think that you're in any position to start laying down conditions.'

'We meet today.'

There was a brief silence. Either she was consulting her diary or – more likely Doug reckoned – she was deliberately making him wait. Then: 'As it happens, I am free today, so let's say 12 at The Masons. I'll bring a memorandum of understanding, just so there can be no confusion over my rights to your story.'

'Of course.'

'See you at 12. The Masons. Don't be late.' She hung up.

'Blimey, Doug, was that wise? After what she wrote about you?' Becca had been standing close by, listening intently. 'If you do prove Mick innocent, it could be a very lucrative story.'

He shrugged. 'Yes, but it will give her an incentive to be a lot more helpful than anyone else has so far been.' In any case, he told himself, at that moment proving Mick was innocent seemed a very long shot indeed.

Doug left for Camelford at 11.15, which was more than enough time to get there and have a look round before walking into the pub at 12 sharp. He was aware of his OCD tendencies when it came to meeting clients, but army habits are not easy to discard, and his being on time was a quality which other people seemed to value – even if they didn't demonstrate it themselves. Becca occasionally teased him about it. What was worse, sometimes she delayed him so much that they arrived at places significantly late. But today she had remained in Bude. Naomi had agreed to meet her at the small department store in town during her lunch break, to help her choose some maternity clothes.

It was raining hard in Camelford, so Doug ended up walking into the pub at 11.55. The woman behind the bar, all black clothes, hair and make-up in the style of Amy Winehouse, pointed a silver-nailed finger towards the corner of the room.

He made his way across the room. The woman there was engrossed in her laptop.

'Ms Kipling?' Doug said quietly. 'I'm Doug.'

She finished typing whatever it was she was typing, then closed the screen down and looked up at him. 'Candice,' she said, in a voice which betrayed years of smoking. 'Let's get our orders in, and then we can talk.' She paused. 'Once you have signed the paperwork, of course.'

Doug sat down. He had been mulling things over ever since he had left Bude. Was this a stupid idea? What questions should he ask her? There were several, but one stood out and needed to be asked first. 'Can I trust you?' he said.

She look back at him. He had, he thought, taken her somewhat off guard. 'Ah,' she said. 'I think you have been reading my piece about Josie.'

'Yes.'

'I was merely using the information I was given.'

'Did you check it out?'

'I got it from a reliable resource.'

'You mean a detective involved with the investigation?'

'I mean exactly what I said. Besides, I am not responsible for what people tell me. It is my job to write a story based on what I learn from a variety of sources.'

'Even if it is lies and unprovable.'

'How can one tell what it is at the time? One asks questions. One listens. One makes judgements. But the truth only comes out in court, when guilt is proven beyond all reasonable doubt.' She paused. 'Or not, as the case may be.'

She passed a single piece of A4 paper, densely typed, to him. He read it slowly.

'So are you going to sign it?'

'Maybe.'

'Yes or no.'

'Maybe after the meal. Not otherwise.'

She laughed, guttural and harsh. 'Playing hard ball are you?'

'Call it what you want. Meal or no meal?'

It was only when they had each ordered a drink and their food – scampi and chips for him and a lasagne and salad for her – that they started talking to each other again.

'You probably think I'm a funny sort of crime reporter,' she began. This comment, Doug decided, was because of her attire. Dressed in a country tweed jacket with a dusky green jumper and matching headband, Doug had already speculated with himself whether under the table she was wearing green wellies or brown country boots. She wasn't pretty. A sharp nose dominated her face, her eyes were an unflinching grey, and overall she came across as a rather formidable, no-nonsense character. 'I do enjoy reporting on crime, but when you work for the local rag, you end up being every sort of reporter: crime, the arts, countryside and even religion. But what I love writing about now are the county shows, the horse racing, the gymkhanas, anything to do with horses or dogs in fact. It's amazing how many invitations I get as a consequence to big houses and fancy shows – free entrance, free food, the best seats and a surprising number of presents turning up on my doorstep at Christmas time. If I am nice to them and give them a good write-up, then they are very nice to me.'

Doug nodded. She felt somewhat alien to him, but he tried not to show it.

'Anyway, I assume you want me to spill the beans on the Layla Lark case, but I am not sure there's a lot to spill. I wrote about it all at the time, and I dare say you've read all my reports, which is why you contacted me. Much as I would love you to prove that there was a miscarriage of justice, so that I can get the exclusive story on it, the case seemed pretty open and shut to me.'

She took a swig of her large glass of red wine and smiled.

'Actually,' Doug said, 'I was particularly interested in the story you wrote about how Detective Sergeant Gooch discovered his boss hanging in his garage.'

She frowned. 'Oh. And why would that be?'

'Well, it was very well written. A detective's worst day ever. But it didn't cover the key question. Why did Duke kill himself?'

'Some sort of mental health issue. I am not quite sure what. Depression I assume. I seem to recall his GP had put him on a mood stabiliser, lithium carbonate I expect, but either that didn't work or he stopped taking it.'

'In one of your other reports, you mention that Duke left no suicide note.'

'That's right. The coroner referred to it in his summing up.'

'That's very unusual.'

'If you say so. Suicide is not one of my areas of expertise.'

'Did you ask Gooch about it?'

'He just said there wasn't one. I didn't need to prompt him with questions. He just opened his mouth and didn't stop talking until he had finished. All I had to do was leave my recorder running.'

'You state in your piece how upset he was when recalling that morning. Do you feel that was genuine or was he putting on an act?'

'An act? Are you serious?' She stared at Doug. 'God, the guy was recalling a really traumatic incident, finding his long-time colleague hanging from the rafters of his garage. It would be odd in my book if he wasn't upset.'

'And it would, in my book, be very strange if a man like Duke had not left a note for his poor wife to read, to explain why he could not live with himself anymore.'

'So what are you saying? That this wasn't suicide?'

'Gooch was first on the scene. He forced entry into the house, supposedly on his way to work in the morning. Who's to say that he didn't actually come to the house in the middle of the night, and then threaten Duke with a gun, force him up onto a chair in the garage and compel him to put his head in a noose—'

'Hey, hey, hey! Your imagination is running away with itself. The pathologist certainly didn't see any reason to suppose it wasn't suicide. And, frankly, if Gooch had wanted to murder him, it would surely have been much easier to summon him to a meeting on the coast – between Bude and Widemouth Bay for example – and then push him over the edge.'

'OK,' Doug said, reluctantly acknowledging the sense in what she was saying. 'But the missing suicide note bothers me. I just don't see him killing himself without leaving a message for his wife.'

'I expect it happens sometimes. People are different. There's no rulebook for how to behave when you're about to kill yourself.' Her tone was dismissive, and they both fell silent.

Shortly afterwards their food appeared. The smell made Doug aware of how hungry he was and he ate three or four mouthfuls before he paused, and raised his fork to get her attention. 'This is my theory. I can't prove it, but I think it is very possible, maybe even probable, that Gooch found the suicide note and destroyed it.'

'Why would he have done that?'

'Because it was incriminating.'

Candice put her cutlery down. Doug had got her attention.

'In what way might it have been incriminating, Doug?'

Doug sighed. 'Mick Raglan insists he wasn't the killer. He thinks he was fitted up. Maybe he got in touch with Duke, threatened or begged him, and Duke finally couldn't live with the guilt any more. So if he left a suicide note, it would have been to admit his own failure, that he knew Raglan wasn't the killer. So when Gooch found him hanging in his garage and found the suicide note, he had—'

'He had to destroy it,' Candice said, finishing for him, 'because he was as guilty as Duke in getting Raglan convicted to life imprisonment.'

'You agree then?'

'No, Doug, I don't. It's a great story, but without

any evidence it gets us nowhere.'

Doug noted her use of 'us' rather than 'you'. It demonstrated that whatever she might say, she was interested in the case.

Later, when they had both devoured their main courses, and then were setting about their sticky toffee puddings – Candice clearly believed in getting her money's worth out of a situation – he posed a question which had been bothering him for some time.

'Did you ever get a sense that Layla had a boyfriend at the time of her death?'

'A sense?' She shrugged. 'The police never said so. But if you talked to the locals, as I did, the general view was that she was pretty and popular in her school—'

'You mean popular with the boys?'

'Yes. But there was no particular boyfriend.'

'Did you not think that was a bit surprising at the time?'

Candice cleaned up the last piece of her pudding and leaned back, replete. 'What you have to remember, Doug, is that people didn't want to speak ill of her. Mick Raglan had been identified as the killer, and that fitted in with people's preconceptions. So why would they want to talk ill of Layla or indeed anyone else?'

'You mean to save Roxanne Lark's feelings?'

'Precisely.'

'I get that.'

'So we've finished eating. Are you going to sign that memorandum?'

'I'm going to make you this verbal commitment. If I prove Mick Raglan innocent, I will give you an exclusive interview for free. The only circumstances in which I will not do so is if you in the meantime write an article in which you make references about me which I deem untruthful.'

'Nothing binding then. Just your word as a gentleman.'

'I've never been a gentleman. But I am a man of my word. Anyway, if you want the scoop—'

He left the words hanging in the air. And she drummed what may have been a tune on the table.

'I suppose I'll just have to trust you?'

'Yes.'

She nodded. 'OK.'

'Coffee?'

Doug was on what had already become his favourite pre-breakfast walk, forcing himself up towards the Storm Tower as best he could. From there he would be able to admire again the panoramic view along the coast and feel the wind in his hair. Not that he ever let his hair get very long, and in any case the wind of the previous day had done a disappearing act. The air was cold, but the clear sky was a promise of a fine day to come. He had left Becca fast asleep in their bed. Rex was running joyfully off the lead in front of him. And he himself was walking sufficiently fast to give himself a bit of a cardiovascular workout, so much so that when his mobile rang, he was puffing audibly.

He stopped, and wondered not for the first time why on earth he hadn't got round to changing the annoying

116

ring tone which his new phone had come with.

'Becca?' he said, ramming it to his ear. But it wasn't her.

'Actually, it's Candice.'

'Oh, sorry. I thought it must be …'

'Your partner? Because why would anyone else be ringing you at this ridiculously early time of day?'

'Something like that.'

'Have you made any progress?'

'As in, have I identified the real killer or found evidence that proves Raglan was innocent?'

She laughed. 'Not exactly. It was more a politeness before I tell you something that might be of interest.'

'I'm listening.'

'This may be an irrelevance. It may not even be true. And I don't want to be responsible for messing up someone's life but …'

'Now that you've rung me and got me interested, you'd better just tell me. I am not a bull-in-the-china-shop detective when I do my investigating.'

'When you're a journalist, people say things. Of course you have to check these things out, not just accept them as being the gospel truth and publish. Otherwise you will sooner or later end up on the wrong end of a legal letter. Anyway, I've been looking through my old notebooks from around that time. It is still one of the biggest stories I've reported on, so I've never felt able to consign them to the recycling bin. Anyway, what I am trying to say is that one person told me this. I am not quite sure whether to believe it or not, but it might be important.'

'OK. You'd better tell me.'

So she did, and at the end of it, before he could ask her any questions, she said she had to go and she killed the phone call. Doug stood very still, staring out to sea for some time, so long in fact that Rex came trotting back from his adventures, sat down at his feet and looked obediently up at him as if to say his walk time was over and breakfast was next. Doug eventually got the message, clipped the lead onto his harness and headed back down the slope.

Doug was uncertain about how to handle the conversation, but he knew it was something that he needed to do, so the sooner the better. Becca had eaten her breakfast and disappeared upstairs to shower and dress. Naomi was clearing up in the kitchen. She had a four-hour shift starting at 10.30. 'Better than nothing,' she said, 'and all thanks to your Becca. I should hang on to her if I were you.'

'Naomi, I need to ask you something.'

'Ask away.' She was full of good humour.

'You might not like it.'

She stopped wiping the work surface and faced him, setting her hands on hips like a fishwife preparing to take on a difficult customer. 'So?'

'Tell me about your brother.'

'Joshua? What about him?'

'Did he like Layla?'

She didn't reply immediately. Doug didn't hold that against her. After all, he had fired his question at her out of the blue. That was enough to throw anyone off balance. But he couldn't help noticing her hesitation, and wondering what might lie behind it. It was as if she needed a few moments to come up with a convincing answer.

'Lots of boys liked her. Haven't I already told you that?'

'I'm interested in Joshua, not the other boys. Now I think about it, I realise that you seem to have deliberately avoided talking about him, full stop. So let me spell it out very simply. Were Joshua and Layla at any stage and in any way boyfriend and girlfriend?'

She shook her head. Then, just in case it hadn't been clear enough, she said, 'No.'

'I've been told the opposite.'

'Who said so? They are lying.'

'I am not going to say who said so. But that is what I was told, which means that I have to consider it. And I also have to consider the possible implications of any such relationship.'

She stared at him for some time before answering. 'What are you saying? That you think my brother killed Layla?'

'No. I am not saying that. But, for example, if he and Layla were an item, then this might have provoked jealousies. After all, as you and others have said, she tended to attract a lot of attention from the opposite sex. Maybe it was like stags fighting for the prize hind in the rutting season. Maybe she liked the idea of being fought over and it all got out of hand.'

'OK.' She ran her hands through her hair before walking across to the table and slumping down in one of the chairs. 'I went into his bedroom one day. I didn't think he was back from school and I wanted to borrow one of his CDs and there they both were. He was naked and she was … well it wasn't the whole thing, but she was making sure he had a good time.'

She was breathing heavily, as if the memory was traumatic.

'Layla would only have been fifteen – at the most.' His words slipped softly out of his mouth, with all their implications.

'What are you saying?' Her reply was sharp and defensive. 'That it was illegal? Look, they weren't actually doing it.'

'Not copulating you mean. At the time you walked in.'

'Right. Later, he begged me not to say anything, not to let on even that Layla had been to the house. Of course, why would I let on to my parents? We agreed it never happened, and then after a few weeks it became obvious to me that they weren't an item any more. She had had her fun and had moved on.'

'And how did Joshua take it? Being dumped at that age – at any age – can be very difficult.'

'That's where you've got it wrong. He was …' Naomi struggled to find the right word. 'He was relieved. It was like he was no longer in her power.'

'How can you be sure?'

'I know my brother. He was much happier after that. He threw himself into sport. He really liked rugby. He told me that it was much less complicated than sex.'

'Thank you.'

'You won't tell the police will you? Or anyone else?'

'No.'

'Because if you do, I will deny it. Everything I have said is off the record.'

'I am not the police. I don't keep records. I just want to find out who killed Layla.'

'Well it wasn't Joshua.'

Doug nodded, as if he accepted what she had said, but inevitably doubt hung around at the back of his brain. How could Naomi know that Joshua wasn't involved? And was it really the case that Joshua was relieved when his relationship with Layla had ended? Doug had a flashback to Joshua grabbing hold of Naomi in the street, insisting she abandon Doug and go off with him. Would a young man like him really have accepted without rancour being dumped by the girl who may well have been given him his first sexual experience. Doug was not convinced.

'How are you?' Zoe said.

Raglan's face expanded into a smile. 'All the better for seeing you, darling.'

'I'm not your darling,' she said sharply.

His face fell. 'Sorry, Jennie.'

'Zoe,' she snapped. 'I am not Jennie any more, and I never will be.'

Zoe wasn't happy to be back in the hospital facing her father. When the bus had dropped her off, she had very nearly got onto another one which would have taken her straight back to the railway station. If Doug Mullen had not rung her up and insisted, she would never have set off to see her father in the first place. But he had been insistent. 'I can't find the truth if you refuse to help me,' he had said. She had told him that he was being manipulative. He had said he was sorry if that was how she saw it. In the end he had convinced her, and so now here she was sitting in full view of her father's gaze, wishing she could be somewhere else – anywhere else except here.

'Sorry!' He was holding up a hand in surrender, and she, despite herself, was feeling something that might have been a mixture of pity and pain. He was sitting in the chair next to his bed. His face was grey, worse than last time, his hair was sparse, there were brown stains on his pyjamas (tea she supposed) and biscuit crumbs on his lap. And yet she could see that there was still a slight sparkle in his eyes.

'Am I allowed to say how very pleased I am to see you?' he said.

She nodded.

'I don't get visitors, except for a priest who comes round and asks me if I have any sins to forgive. And because I have nothing better to do, I start to list them. Being a rubbish father. Punching a guy who tried it on when I was in the showers. Ruining your mother's life. Spitting into someone's food because he said something disrespectful about you. I keep listing them big and small, but that isn't what he wants to hear me say. He wants me to confess that I murdered Layla, but I cannot confess to something I didn't do.'

He had spoken quickly, breathlessly, but now that he had finished he collapsed into a coughing fit.

When he had recovered he asked if she had heard anything from Doug Mullen. 'I hope he's actually doing something for his money.'

'Yes, he is. In fact he asked me to come and see you.'

'There's news then?'

'Not really. It's just that he wants me to ask you something.'

'OK.'

'You may not like the question.'

He was watching her intently, eyes still. 'What's the question?'

'You have to promise to answer it honestly.'

He nodded.

'I want to hear you say it.'

'I promise,' he said. 'I promise to answer you honestly.'

'Mr Mullen wants to know if, while you lived in Bude, you slept with anyone apart from my mother.'

'Are you serious?'

'Answer the question. Yes or no!'

His grey face drained of the little colour left in. He scratched feebly at his stubble. 'No, I didn't.'

She stared at him, unconvinced.

'I promise you, on your mother's grave.'

'You haven't seen my mother's grave, and I'll never tell you where it is. She won't want to listen to your lies.'

He leaned back in his chair. His face seemed to crumple, and although he shut his eyes, tears crept out of them, dribbling down his cheeks. Zoe felt a twinge of guilt, but she hadn't finished.

'So you were totally loyal to Mum?'

'Is that another of Mullen's questions?'

'It's *my* question, she snapped. 'Did you ever try it on with another woman in Bude. Maybe while Mum was pregnant with me?'

He stretched out to get his glass, but knocked it over. Zoe picked it up quickly, filled it with more water, and gave it to him. She knew it wasn't reasonable, but she couldn't help thinking that spilling his water was him was procrastinating again, playing for time, trying not to answer.

'Well?' she demanded.

'I got quite … quite friendly with Judy Trent.'

'What do you mean by "quite friendly"? A hug? A kiss?'

'Yes. Once or twice.'

'Did you feel her tits? Did she give you a blow job?'

He stared back at her. There was sweat on his forehead. Zoe had a sudden premonition that this was going to be the last time she saw her father, and that every time she remembered him it would be this tawdry discussion of his sex life that would fill her mind.

'I … I … I admit that she did once let me feel her breasts. Not let. She encouraged me, undid her blouse. But the other, no. Look, it had been a long day, and she gave me a drink when I returned from my last food delivery and things did get a bit out of hand. But we stopped. We both knew it was wrong and we agreed it shouldn't happen again.'

'Did you tell Mum?'

'No, of course not. I mean, what good would it have done? And I really did want to be a good dad for you when you were born.'

'So that was when Mum was pregnant. You couldn't restrain yourself.' Zoe gripped the arms of her chair, ready to get up and leave. But a woman with breezy manner and a flat Midlands accent came in and gave them each a cup of tea and a biscuit, so she felt compelled to sit for a little longer with her father, this man she barely knew and yet who had in his absence – and now in his presence – dominated her life.

'You've got to believe me. People make mistakes sometimes. I am not a saint. But I promise you we didn't take it any further.'

Zoe said nothing, concentrating on her tea. Twice she looked up and twice she was disconcerted to see that he was peering at her.

In the end she could stick it no longer. She drained what was left of her tea and stood up. She needed to get out, to get away from him. She felt locked in, claustrophobic, as if at any moment she might not be able to breathe any more.

'God, you are like your mother,' he said. 'You know, when you walked in, it was like the first time I saw her.'

She refused to look at him. She didn't trust him further than she could spit. She had already discovered in her short life how people used words as a tool to charm and deceive. She wasn't going to be fooled now.

'Zoe,' he said suddenly. 'Can I ask you something?'

She said nothing. She had run out of words. But he asked her the question anyway. And it was so outrageous that she thought she would faint. She had to grab the back of the chair and hold herself there until she had recovered. Then she straightened herself up, pulled on her coat and walked out, without a parting word or a glance backwards. She stamped angrily along the corridor and down the stairs, and didn't pause until she was outside. She pulled out her vape and sucked on it three or four times. 'How dare he,' she said out loud, oblivious of a couple standing only a few feet away, smoking. 'How bloody dare he!'

It was only when Zoe had got home and demolished three gin and tonics that she felt able to ring Doug, but it wasn't Doug who answered, it was a woman.

'I want to speak to Mr Mullen,' she demanded, the drink exaggerating her mood and volume.

'Mr Mullen is taking a shower. It's quite late,' the woman said pointedly.

'Are you his girlfriend?'

'I am not,' she said firmly. 'I am his partner. I am going to have his baby. My name is Becca, and perhaps you would like to tell me your name.'

The woman's unflustered manner only provoked Zoe all the more. She took a slug of her fourth drink. 'I'm Zoe. Are you saying I can't speak to your *partner* until the morning, even though your *partner* insisted that I had to visit my bloody father? So that is what I have been doing. And right now I need to tell your wonderful *partner* all about it.'

'Didn't it go well, Zoe?'

'What do you mean?'

'I was thinking that maybe the meeting hadn't been very easy for you.'

'What are you? Some sort of cut-price therapist?'

'A humble accident and emergency nurse, actually. But I am also a human being who understands that people sometimes get very stressed by their situations.'

'Do you know what my father asked me to do when I was leaving him today?' She paused momentarily, but only to draw breath. 'My murdering, two-timing father asked me to kiss him, like we were all playing happy families and he had never ruined my life. What do you think of that, Ms Human Being?' But she didn't pause to hear what Becca thought of it. 'Just tell Mr Mullen that I want to speak to him. Now.'

'I can see you did find the meeting difficult, so listen, Zoe, and listen carefully because I am going to say this once, and once only. I want you to stop drinking alcohol – if that is what you are drinking – and make yourself a nice mug of tea or cocoa. Then at any time between 10.30 and eleven this evening you can ring back again and talk to Mr Mullen, though I am sure he will be happy if you call him Doug. But what neither of us are prepared to tolerate is verbal or other abuse. Do I make myself clear?'

Zoe was speechless. Who the hell did this woman think she was? Why couldn't she just go and drag the man out of the shower. She was paying him, after all.

'So I am now going to terminate this phone call, Zoe, and I hope that in half an hour you will be in a calmer state and will feel able to ring back and have a sensible conversation with Doug. Good bye.'

And that was it.

Zoe stood rock still, a frozen statue, and then hurled her glass against the wall, so that the remains of the drink sprayed a wild pattern over the magnolia wall. 'Damn you,' she yelled into the void of her own pain, before going in search of another glass.

CHAPTER SIX

I<small>T WAS NEARLY</small> 8.30, and Doug and Becca were eating breakfast in silence. It was a frosty rather than companionable one because Zoe Finch had not rung back the night before. Doug had initially admired Becca for standing up to her the previous evening, but now his attitude had changed and he had spent several minutes quizzing Becca on what exactly she had said to Zoe and how come she had been so 'forthright' that Zoe hadn't rung back.

'I don't care if you're working for her,' she said firmly. 'I won't take abuse in the workplace, and I won't take it from anyone over the telephone. And nor should you.'

'Suppose she doesn't ring back?'

'She will.'

'How do you know?'

'Because she needs to talk to you. About her father. And because of what he said to her and because one way or another she needs to know if he is a killer. Now let's have a nice calm breakfast.'

'She can only be eighteen or nineteen. You should have made allowances.'

'No I shouldn't.'

There were footsteps on the stairs. 'Everything all right?' It was Naomi. How long had she been hovering on the landing, listening. 'I'm sorry, bad timing is it?'

'No,' they said in unison.

'I'm in the way. I know that. A house should be a place where you can have a good old-fashioned row and clear the air, but when you've got a stray woman hanging around …'

'It's OK,' said Doug the peacemaker

'I just wanted a cup of tea, and then I'll skedaddle back upstairs.'

'We weren't arguing about you,' Becca added. 'If we had been, I would tell you straight. Now make yourself a cuppa and join us.' She made it sound like an order.

Doug settled into a slightly bolshy silence. His phone was on the table, and his eyes constantly glanced at it as if it might suddenly disappear into thin air and then all would be lost. By contrast the two women settled into a desultory and somewhat wary chatter, exchanging small talk about the restless night they had each had – neither had slept well – and the early-morning noise of the gulls, and the best place to buy proper free-range eggs.

Finally Doug raised his eyes and focused on Naomi. She turned, conscious of his attention.

'Tell me about Mick Raglan's wife.'

'Greta, you mean.'

'Yes.'

'She was OK. Scandinavian blood, I guess. Blonde, quite muscular, helped out with the surfing and the swimming club.'

'And they had a daughter.'

'Yeah. Jennie. Quite cute. I remember her toddling around on the beach, but then mother and child disappeared once Mick has been arrested. Too difficult to be here after that. I guess.'

'Greta is dead.'

'Oh. I didn't realise.'

'One of the things I've been running through my head is whether Greta might have got involved with someone else, and if so whether that might have been a reason why Mick was framed for Layla's murder.'

'But Mick was seen with Layla the night she died. That's why he was found guilty. Hell, it was Josie who saw the two of them together there.'

'And now Josie is dead.'

Naomi frowned, and pointed her cereal spoon at Doug. 'Are you saying Josie lied? Why would she have done that? She wasn't like that.'

'I am not saying she was lying. I am merely wondering why, once I arrived and started asking awkward questions, someone in this town decided that it was vitally important to make sure that Josie was silenced. Was there something she knew that would have proved that Mick didn't kill Layla? Maybe she knew something, but just wasn't aware of its significance.'

'So you think whoever killed Josie also killed Layla.'

'Well it is either that or a deliberate copycat killing.'

Naomi lowered her spoon, and began to eat her cereal.

But Doug had not finished. 'I know you were only fifteen at the time, and I don't want to be a nag, but you must have seen a bit of Greta as well as Mick. Do you remember anything that, in retrospect, makes you think that Greta had admirers?'

And that was when Doug's phone rang.

'This is Zoe, Mr Mullen,' a voice said.

'Thank you for ringing back,' Doug said.

'Last night, I was out of order.'

'So I gather.'

'I found my flatmate's gin and well … things got out of hand.'

'Alcohol does that sometimes. Someone once told me "Drink because you are happy, but never because you are miserable". I think he was quoting someone famous. I find it is good advice.' Doug paused, conscious that he was sounding like a wise old fart.

'Please apologise to your partner. She tells me you are going to be a dad.'

'Yes.'

'Be a good one. Whatever else you do in life, be a good dad. There is nothing more important for a man.' Now it was her scattering gnomic wisdom all over him.

'I intend to be a very good dad,' he reassured her. 'Mine was rubbish.'

'There's a train that will get me to Okehampton at 2.15. Is there any chance of you meeting me there?'

'You want to come to Bude?' Doug had never met her, but when they had first spoken on the phone, she had insisted she would never ever go to Bude herself.

'I don't want to. But I can't talk about him over the phone, and I have to tell you what he said. Besides I …' She stumbled into silence.

'I'll pick you up,' Doug said, wondering what the besides might have been. 'There are three bedrooms, so plenty of space in the house.'

'Thank you.'

'Just one rule,' he said. 'No alcohol.'

Doug heard a rueful laugh. 'I still have a hangover.'

The drive from Okehampton to Bude was quiet. Within five minutes, Zoe had fallen asleep, and Doug had to put on hold any thoughts of getting an update from her. The most striking thing about her was her likeness to her mother. There were a few press photos of Greta in his collection, and you could not miss the likeness – the blonde curly hair, the strong square face, and eyes that stared boldly out at the world. Mother and daughter had changed their names when they had left Bude, but that was all.

Like a dog which automatically wakes up as soon as the destination hoves into sight, Zoe rubbed her eyes as they turned off the Atlantic Highway and headed down towards the town centre and the sea.

'Do you remember Bude, at all?' he asked.

'No,' she said. 'I was only two.' Mostly that was true, except that she could recall being carried on a man's back across a sandy beach. And that, she presumed, must have been Bude.

'We have an extra person in the house,' Doug said. 'Apart from my partner Becca, that is. Her name is Naomi, and she was a friend of Layla, and she is staying with us because she is afraid.'

'Why is she afraid?'

'Because two days ago someone called Josie Archer was murdered. It is possible that her death and Layla's are connected.'

'Oh my gosh,' she gasped. 'Why didn't you warn me?'

'Well we've not spoken much have we. And I suppose I was focusing on other things. Josie was a close friend of Naomi and Layla. Anyway, Naomi is a bit scared and I want to make sure she stays safe.'

'Perhaps I shouldn't have come. Suppose they want to kill me?'

'You were a very young child.'

'I'm the daughter of a killer. If they find out who I am, maybe I'll be next.'

'Try not to panic. No-one knows you.'

But you can't stop someone panicking just by telling them not to. Zoe was in full scale alarm mode. 'I need to change my appearance,' she wailed. 'I've seen photos of my mum when she was younger. Everyone used to say how alike we were. Someone will recognise me and then it will be all round the town and—'

'We'll change your appearance. Naomi can help.'

'Naomi?' Disbelief was written large across her face. 'How?'

'She's a hairdresser. She can cut and colour your hair, straighten it too. No-one will link you to your mother or to the little girl of two who once lived here. Trust me. I will keep you safe.' *Trust me. I will keep you safe*. How on earth could he promise her that?

'There,' said Naomi. 'What do you think?'

The transformation was startling. Zoe looked in the mirror and couldn't quite believe it. Straight auburn hair styled in a bob, eyebrows straightened, skin pale and interesting. It wasn't quite her, and she didn't particularly like the result, but she certainly looked like a different woman. 'You need a hat and more flattering clothes, but apart from that you'll do. People may look at you, but not because they recognise you.'

'I'll need to have a chat with Zoe at some point,' Doug said, and like a morning mist both Becca and Naomi were gone, slipping out of the front door to go and pick up a supper.

'So what did you find out from your father?'

'He said he never had an affair with anyone else in Bude.'

'Do you believe him?'

'I don't know. You see, he admitted he got quite close to a woman called Judy Trent—'

'Naomi's mother.'

'Oh my God. I didn't realise! We mustn't tell her.'

'Definitely not.'

'He said they didn't go through with things. Got pretty close as far as I can tell, but my mum was pregnant with me and … and …'

'And they both felt guilty maybe.'

'I hope so.'

They both fell silent. Outside gulls screeched, and the wind rattled a tin can gaily down the road.

'He said he stopped because he wanted be a good father.'

'I can understand that.'

'The bastard wanted to kiss me goodbye.' She rubbed at her eyes which were moist and red. Doug got up and passed her the box of tissues from the coffee table.

She stared up at him. 'Can you believe that, Mr Mullen? After all that's happened.'

'Actually, I can,' he said softly. 'People are complicated. And please, do call me Doug.'

Doug looked at his watch. 'I think it's time to be going.'

The three women looked at him and stood up as one. He had not intended them to accompany him, but once he had mentioned his plan, there had been no stopping them. As Naomi had said, 'We don't want to miss out.'

There was a last minute trip to the toilets for all of them, and then they were pulling on coats, wrapping scarves, and lacing on boots. Rex sat disconsolately in his basket. He had already been offered a chance to cock his leg out the back, and he knew from experience that he would not be welcome on the forthcoming outing. Doug tossed him a biscuit and shut the door firmly behind him.

Outside they split into pairs. Naomi and Zoe had already developed a bond. They linked arms and strode out, leaving Doug and Becca to follow at a more sedate pace. They crossed the canal, passed the car park and tourist centre on the right, and walked as far as the roundabout before looping left along the Strand, the River Neet on their left.

'Doug, are you OK?' Becca said.

He shrugged and glanced sideways at her. 'Do you think this is a complete waste of time?'

She was his rock, and he needed her reassurance. She took his hand, squeezed it for a few seconds, then released him.

Naomi and Zoe slowed down as they drew near to the bus stop, then stopped a few metres away from it.

Naomi glanced back at Doug and waited for him to take the lead.

'This is where Josie Archer saw Mick Raglan talking to Layla Lark. It was this time of year, about 8.30 on a Friday evening.' He spoke with the precision of a tourist guide who had gained his blue badge. 'Unlike tonight, it was cloudy, dry but darker than it is now. According to Josie's testimony, Mick offered her a cigarette and then helped her light it.'

'So Mick was a smoker, Naomi?'

'Yeah.'

'And how much did Layla smoke?' Becca was asking the questions. It was what she and Doug had agreed.

'Not a lot. But she would cadge them off people.'

'So you think that was what she was doing that night. Cadging a cigarette and a light off Mick?'

'I guess so.'

'Would she normally be out in town at this time of night?'

'It depends.'

'On what?'

'On whether her mum was at home, monitoring when she came in.'

'And was her mum at home that night?'

'I dunno. You'd have to ask her.'

'So why might Layla have come to this bus stop?'

'If you want to meet someone, there's good cover from the rain. And the wind too.' As if to prove her point, a sudden gust whipped over them.

Doug stepped forward in front of the group and turned to face Naomi. 'What about you, Naomi? Did you ever meet people here? At this time of night?'

She hesitated, caught off guard by the sudden personal question. 'Sometimes, if I was going out. But not as late as this.'

'Who would you meet here?'

'Mates.'

'Boy mates or girl mates?'

'Girls mostly.'

'Like Layla and Josie, you mean?'

'Yeah. Them and others.'

'You see,' Doug continued, 'I stand here and look around, and I think it's a good place for meeting mates, but if you wanted to meet someone secretly, then this would not be the place I'd choose. This bus stop is at the bottom of the main street, in full view of pubs and takeaways, people smoking outside, people out walking down to the beach with their dogs or across the river and down to the canal. There's a sports place over there.' He pointed across the river. 'This is not a good place for a nice discreet rendezvous. So if Layla was intending to meet someone here, then my guess it was someone she knew well and it was someone she wasn't reluctant to be seen with.'

'But we know she met my father here.' They were the first words that Zoe had spoken since they had left the cottage, and they brought home sharply that this was no game. For her, this was very, very personal.

'Yes, Zoe, we do. But maybe that was by chance.' He paused, measuring his words with care. 'Maybe she was waiting here to meet someone else. But your father saw her on her own and went over and offered her a cigarette, and then, maybe, after a chat, he moved on. So the question in my head is this. If she wasn't waiting for Mick, then who was it? Did that person ever turn up? And if that person was just a "mate", then how come they never came forward and made a statement?'

No-one responded, and it was Becca who took charge. 'Let's move on, Doug. It's too cold for standing around and frankly it's a bit spooky.'

He nodded, and they set off again, this time with him in the lead, heading along Summerleaze Crescent, past the public car park which served the beach, and up onto the top. From there it took only two or three more minutes to reach the edge of the headland. They stopped and looked down at the sea pool. Becca took Zoe's hand and held it tight. God only knew what the girl was feeling right now, to be seeing for the first time the place where her father was alleged to have murdered a schoolgirl.

Doug moved back into tour guide mode: 'Layla died here at some time in the later evening or early morning. Her body wasn't discovered until a little after six o'clock in the morning by a dog walker. She was lying face down in the pool, still wearing her clothing, including her coat and trainers. There was some damage to her dress, but no sign that she had been raped or indeed had had consensual sex. There was severe bruising on her head, but she died of drowning.'

Becca shivered. 'You wouldn't come up here at that time of year in the dark with someone you didn't know. And I can't imagine she would have come up here on her own, with some stalker following her.'

'You might if you had arranged to meet someone here,' Doug said.

Zoe began to whimper, and Becca responded by wrapping her arms around her. 'Doug, for crying out loud, let's get home. We've had more than enough.'

'The tide is out. We can cross the beach and save some time.' He switched on his torch and directed them down the steps, past the pool and then down onto the sand. That was when, from somewhere high up behind them, someone shouted.

All four of them turned. That's what people do in such circumstances. It is a normal human reaction to look to see who and what and why. But an unwise one when someone is hurling stones down onto you. The first of them struck Doug on the shoulder. It was hard and heavy, and he yelled at the others to run. There was another shout from one of the shadows in the darkness above them, this time of glee at having hit the target. Doug heard the harsh grunts as more stones were being launched. He looked around. He could see the outline shapes of Becca and Zoe struggling across the sand, but Naomi was close to him and was standing stock still, staring up into the dark, mesmerised by what was unfolding.

'Run,' he shouted, but it was too late. One stone hurtled so close to him that he could feel its slipstream, and then another hit its mark. Naomi's arms seemed to fling themselves into the air. He flicked his torch on and swung it around. Becca and Zoe, he saw with relief, were some way distant, hurrying to put even more distance between themselves and their assailants. But Naomi was hurrying nowhere. She was splayed out on the beach, her hands like claws in the sand. He dropped down beside her, saw the unseeing eyes and the blood on the side of her face, and he bellowed across the beach. 'Becca!'

If ever he needed her accident and emergency skills, it was now. As he scrabbled for his phone to dial 999, he looked up into the darkness and thought he saw two dark shadows standing there looking down. But moments later they were running away, and moments after that they had completely disappeared.

CHAPTER SEVEN

Doug returned from a breezy walk along the cliffs feeling worse than when he had started off. He had hoped to clear his mind, but that had been a ridiculous fantasy. How could he clear his mind when Naomi was in critical care and it was all his fault? What had he been thinking of, allowing – no, not allowing, but encouraging – the three women to walk with him as he retraced and revisited Layla's last hours. It was his decision and so his fault.

Why had he not retraced Layla's last steps on his own? Of course, he knew the answer to that. He had wanted Becca's support and wisdom, and he had wanted Naomi there too because she had been a friend of Layla and might therefore be able to get inside Layla's mind in a way no-one else could. In those circumstances he could hardly have refused to allow Zoe to come with them. But those were excuses. It had been his fault, just as Josie's death had been. If he had turned down Raglan's offer of money, if he had stayed in Oxfordshire, then she would almost certainly still be alive. He had come to Bude, and Death had followed him all the way, brandishing His lethal scythe in His bloody hands.

When he re-entered the cottage, it was to find Becca and Zoe up and dressed.

'Any news from the hospital?' he asked.

While they had been at the hospital the previous

evening, Becca had made no secret of her own A & E nursing experience and had succeeded in establishing a rapport with the staff. In particular she had extracted a promise from a nurse called Patience that she would contact her when anything changed in Naomi's condition.

'No news,' Becca said. 'Which I guess is good news.' Despite that, her face was grim. 'Anyway, let's have some breakfast, and decide what we do next.'

It was Zoe who broke the silence as they were eating their porridge. 'Maybe we should stop.'

Becca and Doug looked at each other, then back at her.

'Suppose she dies,' Zoe continued. 'She was really nice to me, and if I hadn't agreed with Dad, then none of this would have happened. Josie or Naomi.' She began to cry, huge sobs which wracked her body. Becca moved to comfort her, but Doug sat there, numb, conscious that it was he and no-one else who had taken Raglan's money and come to Bude.

Eventually, when Zoe was quiet, her hand resting in Becca's firm grip, Doug spoke. 'I am happy to stop – and hand back all the money I have already received – if that is what you want. All I will say is that everything that has happened since we arrived points to the fact that your father was innocent, and that there are people in the town who know that full well. I fear they will do anything to keep the truth buried. I've been attacked, Josie has been murdered, and now Naomi's life in hanging in the balance.'

'Maybe those people last night didn't realise who we were,' Becca said. 'Maybe they were just some yobs who had had a drink too many and thought they would have a bit of fun, only it got out of hand.'

'Oh, I think they knew who we were alright. Not you, Zoe, of course. I think they followed us deliberately. Let me say this. Last night when it all kicked off, Naomi didn't immediately run. You two were in front, doing what any normal people would have done in the circumstances, running as fast as you could. But Naomi didn't. She was just behind me and she turned round and looked up at the top of the cliff. At the time, I assumed that fear had overwhelmed her. But she didn't look terrified. She looked … as if she couldn't believe what was happening.'

'So what's your point, Doug?'

'I wonder if she may have mentioned our plan to someone, told them how we were going to retrace Layla's last steps. That would explain how it was that they were able to wait for us and then follow us.'

'But why would she mention it?'

'Because it didn't seem that big a deal. Because she trusted the person she was speaking to.'

'But who?'

'She was working at the hairdresser again yesterday, wasn't she. Maybe she mentioned it to a customer, though that seems less likely to me. Maybe someone she knows went to find her at the hairdresser to talk to her, and she let the cat out of the bag then.'

'In that case,' Becca said, 'we need to go to the hairdresser and ask some questions.'

Doug nodded. 'There's something else that is bothering me. My assumption was that the stone-throwers were aiming at me, determined to drive me back to Oxford. But walking the cliffs this morning, it occurred to me that maybe, just maybe, it was Naomi who was the target. After all, of the three friends, she is the only one still alive. Perhaps it is she who holds the key to it all.'

DI Jennings knocked on the door and went in. It was immediately obvious that this was not going to be a pleasant experience. Detective Superintendent Hinchcliffe wasn't on his own. Sitting a metre or so away from him was the commissioner, and both of them were looking as though they would happily feed her to the nearest pack of wolves. Neither invited her to sit down, but after some hesitation she did so anyway. 'Stand up for yourself,' her partner Jamila had said that morning, just as she was chivvying their four-year-old out of bed. 'Imagine he's naked. A horrible thought I know, but that technique always works for me.'

'Inspector,' Hinchcliffe said, 'perhaps you would like to bring us up to date with what is going on in Bude. One of the prime tourist spots of our lovely county, yet here as the season looms it has become one of the most dangerous places in England.'

Jennings was having trouble imagining Hinchcliffe naked. Instead, she tried looking him full in the face. 'One death and one serious injury is much less—'

'Don't start splitting hairs with me, Inspector. I know the details. One woman found dead at the bottom of the cliff only a few hundred metres from the famous sea pool, some fifteen years after Layla Lark was murdered there. And not just any woman, but Josie Archer, the woman who testified to seeing Mick Raglan with Lark shortly before her death. Another close friend of Lark's then nearly gets her skull smashed in. And in the middle of all this mess, some self-appointed private investigator has taken money from Lark's killer and is announcing to all and sundry that Mick Raglan did not after all kill Lark.'

Jennings frowned, at which point the commissioner joined in. He tossed a newspaper at her. 'Front bloody page. Makes us, and above all you, look like incompetent fools.' She glanced at it, and the headlines alone made her shudder.

'*One woman dead, one woman in a coma, and Cornwall and Devon's Police Clueless*'

How come no-one in her team had warned her?

'Arrest Mullen, and either charge him or tell him to crawl back under whichever stone he emerged from. Or do you have a better prime murder suspect up your sleeve?'

'Well it can't be Raglan because he's still locked up and has a terminal cancer diagnosis. And Mullen himself was with Naomi when she was hit by a stone.'

'Don't get smart with me, Inspector. Just get on and do your job, and sort it out.' He waved a hand of dismissal. 'Or else.'

When Becca walked into the hairdresser, Kay looked up and scowled. 'You again!'

'Me again.'

'Where the heck is Naomi? I heard what you said and I gave her another chance, and look what happens.

She doesn't turn up. She was meant to be here by 9.15. Ready for a full day's work. But she ain't.'

'That's because she's in hospital.'

'Hospital?' Kay straightened up and gave Becca her full attention. 'Is she ill?'

'Not ill. But she's unconscious, because last night someone hurled a stone at her and hit her full on the head, and right now it's touch and go whether she'll survive.'

'Are you serious?' She seemed genuinely shocked. 'Who would have done that?'

'I need five minutes of your time and I need it in total privacy.'

She glanced up at the clock. 'Ten minutes before my first customer comes. You've got five and not a second longer. But I need to contact one of my other girls first, otherwise I'm going to have some very unhappy customers.' She fiddled around with her mobile, made the call, then slipped it into her pocket. 'Right, what do you want to know?'

'I want to know if Naomi spoke to anyone yesterday who wasn't a customer.'

'Her brother. He called round about lunchtime. She went off with him and came back fifteen minutes later with a coffee and some sort of bun.'

'Where from?'

'I don't know.'

'The coffee cup might have been branded.'

She frowned. 'Costa, I think.'

'Anyone else call in for a chat with her?'

'No. I don't encourage it.' She was, Becca reckoned, a woman, who didn't encourage a lot of things.

'Whose hair did she cut yesterday?'

She went over to her reception desk and picked up a book. 'Take a photo if you like. She did all those marked with an "N".'

'Thanks.'

'Anything else?'

'No, thank you.' Becca made her way to the door.

'I hope you're still pleased with your hair.'

'Yes.'

'Sometimes, a few days later people decide they're not, and they come back and tell me so.'

Becca pulled open the door and looked back at Kay. 'Why is it, do you think, that whenever I ask questions hereabouts, I get the impression that people are only ever telling me half the truth.' She paused, her eyes fixed on Kay. 'Present company excluded, of course.'

Doug was waiting for her outside.

'Costa,' she said.

'You want a coffee while we are there?'

'Might as well.'

Inside Costa, Doug put in their order – a flat white for him and a hot chocolate for her – while Becca took up position in the corner. 'Would you mind bringing it over? I'm a bit unsteady on my pins at the moment,' he said. It was a lie, but in the circumstances and given that his ribs were still feeling sorry for themselves, he felt it was necessary.

A woman brought the drinks over. 'Can I ask you a question?' Becca said as soon she had finished offloading their drinks. 'Do you know Naomi Trent? Your sort of age, works down the hill at the hairdresser.'

'Sure. We were at school together. She was the year above me.'

'She came in here yesterday. With her brother.'

She frowned. 'No, she was on her own. I remember because she doesn't come in here that often, so we had a bit of a chinwag. I served her and then she came and sat down here where you are, with an ex-copper called Gooch. It was only for a few minutes. She didn't even take her coat off, then she headed off with her coffee and croissant.'

'I don't suppose you have any idea what they were talking about?'

She laughed. 'I don't have time to eavesdrop on people's conversations.'

'And does Gooch make a habit of coming in here?'

'You ask a lot of questions. What are you, an undercover copper?' And with that she laughed and returned to the counter to deal with a customer who was kicking off with her young colleague.

They had barely got back to the cottage before there was a rapping on the door.

'That must be Zoe,' Becca said, but when she opened the door, she found herself facing DI Jennings and DS Bristow.

'We need to ask Mr Mullen and yourself a few more questions.'

'You'd better come in.'

They sat down at the table, but no coffee was offered or requested. This was not a time for pleasantries.

'I understand you were with Naomi Trent last night.'

Doug nodded.

'So tell me about it, step by step.'

Doug did just that. He had been revisiting it in his head ever since he had tried to go to sleep the previous night and largely failed. So the details were clear, yet telling the story out loud was an altogether different experience. In the end he just ran out of words.

Becca finished off. 'We spent a couple of hours in the hospital until it was obvious there was nothing to be done by waiting there any longer. That's it.'

'Have you any idea who might have thrown the stones?'

'We didn't recognise them, if that's what you mean. It was dark and frankly we were trying to get the hell out of it.'

'And do you think they were aiming for one of you or just trying to scare you?'

'Are you serious? Are you expecting us to read the minds of some loonies who think pelting people with stones is an acceptable way of spending their evening?'

'From what Mr Mullen has said, he was struck on the shoulder and poor Naomi of course was hit on the head, so it stands to reason—'

'They were closer. Zoe and I were in front and so further away.'

'Is this Zoe staying here, with you?'

'She's out.'

'Do you know where she is or when she will be back?'

'No, and no.' Becca's desire to assist the police with their enquiries was notable only by its absence.

'Is there anything else?' Doug said, finally rejoining the conversation.

Jennings stood up and began to button up her coat. 'Just one thing. Given what has happened to Josie and Naomi, and given that it is your visit here that seems to have been a catalyst for it, my boss has asked me to pass on the suggestion that it might in the circumstances be wisest if you were to cut your stay short and return to Oxford.'

'No.' Becca's reply was whiplash sharp. 'We are staying until I know that Naomi is out of danger.'

'And,' Doug said, 'until we've discovered who actually killed Layla.'

Jennings surveyed them. 'I do understand your feelings. But let me make one thing absolutely clear. If you interfere in any way with our investigations, then we will be hauling you into the station for a lot of hard questions.'

'We have no intention of interfering with your work. But we also have no intention of going home early.'

Doug shut the door behind the two officers with relief. He turned and faced Becca. She was looking at him. 'You OK?' she said.

'No.' He moved forward and slumped down on the chair he had just vacated. 'Maybe this is just too big for us. Maybe she is right. Maybe we should go home and leave them to sort things out.'

'You're not a quitter, Doug.' Her voice was soft, yet urgent. 'Don't start now.'

'I'll let Zoe decide. I'll talk to her again.'

'She won't agree to it.'

'How do you know?' He got up and walked over to the window. He looked out. The clouds were thick and grey, and a substantial drizzle was falling on the surface of the road. 'Anyway,' he said, 'I wonder where she's got to.'

'She'll turn up eventually.'

'Well I can't wait forever. If we do stay, I think I'm going to change tack.'

'Change tack? What exactly does that mean?'

Doug turned to look at her, a wry smile on his face. 'I haven't worked that out yet.'

Sally Duke was sitting in a chair under the covered veranda. It was cool, and she was wearing a crumpled dark green coat that had seen better days, and a scarf and woollen hat.

'There's a gentleman to see you, Sally. His name is Doug.'

Sally turned her head and found herself looking at a man with short hair, a damp grey anorak, and bruised face. 'Do I know you?' she said.

'I'll bring you both a cup of tea and some biscuits,' the carer said, before retreating back into the body of the building.

'Are you warm enough?' Doug said, sidestepping her question. 'We could go inside if you prefer.' Now that he was here, he was unsure about how to proceed. How could he question her without alarming her? What did he hope to get out of meeting DI Duke's widow? What right did he have to be here anyway?

'Do I know you?' she repeated.

'I was in the police force a long time ago. I worked for your husband.' It wasn't the first time Doug had lied in the course of his job. It was a necessity sometimes. But on this occasion and to this old lady, he felt particularly uneasy. His overriding emotion as she looked at him was guilt.

'Doug? I don't recall him talking about anyone called Doug.'

'I was just a constable then.'

'Ah!' She nodded as if him being a constable explained everything.

'There was a sergeant called Gooch too. We all called him Goochie.'

'I didn't like him,' she said decisively. 'Don't want to talk about him.'

'He wasn't everyone's cup of tea down at the station.'

'Tea? I thought that Carla girl was going to bring me some tea. And a biscuit. Chocolate I hope. They like to give you the plain ones, the cheap ones. We pay enough money. I had to sell my house just to be here, so it's not unreasonable to expect chocolate biscuits. Especially when I have a visitor.'

'Here we are!' It was Carla again, bright and breezy, and with perfect timing. 'Managed to find a couple of chocolate biscuits. Just don't tell the others because they are having to settle for rich tea today.'

Carla placed the tray on the low table. 'Now, Sally, you be nice to Doug. He's come a long way to see you. No misbehaving!' And she gave Doug a wink.

They sat in silence for some time, sipping tea. Doug ate his biscuit gratefully, and watched Sally dipping hers in her cup, allowing the chocolate to melt. And in that moment he decided he should make his excuses and go. It had been a stupid idea to come in the first place.

'Can't see what my Danny saw in him,' she said suddenly.

'You mean Detective Sergeant Gooch?'

'Dreadful man.' Apparently Sally had changed her mind about not discussing him. 'Terrible BO and he drank too much.'

'Who had BO and drank too much?'

Doug turned around to see another woman standing there. Fifties, smartly clothed in floral black and white dress and navy jacket, short hair and stern face.

'Darling!' Sally smiled. 'Fancy you coming too.'

The woman leant down and kissed Sally. 'Hello, Mother.' Then she turned her attention to Doug. 'I am Laura, the daughter. And who might you be?'

'I'm Doug. I'm sorry, I've probably outstayed my welcome.'

'But what brings you here?'

Doug stood up. 'It's complicated.'

'Complicated! What exactly does that mean?' Her words were controlled and concise.

'I'll be off now, but if you need to know more, you can ring me.' He opened his wallet, handed her his card, and waited for the explosion.

But there was no eruption of anger, no demand to know who the heck he was and what on earth he was doing here. Instead she studied it in silence for several seconds before slipping it into her pocket and looking him full in the face. 'Why don't you wait in the car park, and I will join you as soon as I can?'

'As soon as I can' turned out to be some forty minutes, by which time Doug was feeling distinctly irritated. Maybe that was her way of establishing that she wasn't a woman to be messed with, and that tea and biscuits with her mother was more important than him – which of course was true. But eventually Laura Duke came striding out of the main entrance, scanned the car park, and beckoned him towards her. Doug gave himself a metaphorical shake and headed towards her, conscious that this was going to be a difficult meeting.

'I lied,' he said. It was better, he hoped, to come clean. 'Lied to the care home and to your mother.'

'Can you be more precise?'

'I was never in the police and I never knew your father.'

She pulled his business card out of her pocket and brandished it. 'Yet you call yourself a private investigator.'

'Because I am.'

'Let me guess. You are the investigator who has been in Bude claiming the Mick Raglan never murdered Layla Lark?'

'Don't believe everything you are told in the press. I have made no precise claims.'

'Either you think he did it or you think he didn't.'

Doug took a deep breath. 'He's dying. He claims to be innocent. I am inclined to think he may be telling the truth.'

'So let me guess. You think there was a police stitch up? And that my father was behind it all?'

'Not a stitch up. A mistake. A genuine mistake, I hope. But I do think there may have been a miscarriage of justice.'

'So you visited my mother to try and extract information that would have shown the world that her husband got it wrong.'

'I am only trying to discover the truth. I asked your mother barely any questions. To be honest, when I sat down to drink tea with her, I was at a loss for words. And the only thing that your mother told me was that she disliked and distrusted DS Gooch.'

'I would agree with her on that.'

'Any particular reason? I believe your father worked with him for some time.'

'Apart from anything else, he was creepy.'

'In what way?'

She shuddered, and she looked around suddenly as if worried that someone or something was watching them. 'Not here,' she said, in little more than a whisper. 'Our house.'

They drove in convoy. Not that it was far to go, a couple of miles and they were there. A semi-detached house with a garage on the right. Laura pulled up in front of it, and Doug next to her.

'Is this where your parents lived?' he asked as he followed her to the front door.

'Yes. It still belongs to my mother. But I may have to sell it. Her care is expensive and …'

'Oh, I thought your mother said it had already been sold to fund the care home.'

She spun round, stopping him in his tracks. 'What is that meant to mean? Are you investigating me too?'

'No, of course not. I guess your mother was confused.'

She opened her mouth to say something more, but apparently changed her mind. Instead she unlocked the front door and went inside. She went straight to the fridge, extracted a half empty bottle of white wine from it, located a glass, filled it up, and took a deep swig.

'Would you like one?'

'I've got to drive back to Bude.'

'A small one then.' Her idea of a small one turned out to be extremely generous, but he accepted it without a murmur and followed her out of the kitchen-diner to a smaller room dominated by a large TV, facing which were two heavily patterned armchairs, each with its own side-table. There was also a beige tiled fireplace on top of which were several family photographs, the central one of which was a black-and-white one of Danny and Sally Duke in wedding attire.

'Sit down,' she ordered, slumping down into the chair on the right. 'OK. Here's the full story of the house. I've told my mother that I sold it so that I don't have to bring her back here. You see, that's what I did at first. I offered to take her out in the car, thinking a visit to a tea shop would be nice, but every time she insisted that she wanted to go and have her tea at home. Then she would decide that she wanted to stay here and not go back to the home. She would get quite aggressive, and I had the devil of a job to persuade her otherwise. So I lie for peace and quiet. Of course, the fact is that the care home is expensive, and so I shall have to put it on the market in the next few months. But in the meantime I've been able to start sorting through all her stuff.'

'I can see all this must have been very difficult for you.'

Doug took a sip of wine. Laura was staring at the wedding photograph of her parents, lost in her thoughts. 'And I was sorry to read about your father.'

She turned and frowned. 'Ah! So you know about that.'

'Candice Kipling wrote a …'

'I know that!' The words are almost a scream. 'She turned my father's death into a celebration of the wonderful DS Gooch. Made him sound like my dad's best friend, a man of huge empathy and sorrow.'

Doug nodded, unable to find any words that might be acceptable.

'We just wanted to mourn him in peace, but fat chance of that with Ms Kipling milking the situation for all she was worth.'

'Back in the car park, you said Gooch was creepy. What did you mean by that?'

'He's one of those men who run their eyes over you rather than looking you in the face. Make unsuitable comments. There are plenty of other guys like that around, of course. But the fact was he made my skin crawl. I think Mother disliked him because she felt he was a bad influence on Father. My father was a nice guy, he was too nice for the job, especially when it came to standing up to the likes of Gooch.

Doug took a sip of his wine, then a second one before carefully putting his glass down on his side-table. 'Do you have any idea why your father … killed himself?'

'He was on pills. For depression.'

'How bad was his depression, because as I understand it he was still working at the time?'

'I wasn't here. I was based in Exeter then. I used to come back when I could, but my life was complicated and messy and …' She fell silent and sipped moodily at her wine before resuming. 'Mother told me he had been on pills for two or three years.'

'And had you noticed any deterioration in his condition?'

'I can't pretend I had. He was on what the doctor called a maintenance dose. The last time his case had been reviewed, they had decided there was no reason to increase it.'

'Did your mother say anything about those last days?'

'Afterwards, it was almost impossible to get her to talk about it. It was such a shock for her. She blamed herself. Her mother had been taken ill, and she had decided she must go up to Leicestershire for a few days and see how she could help. And that was when he did it. If she had stayed at home, she thinks, he would still be alive.'

'This may seem an odd questions, but did she drive there?'

Laura frowned. 'Well, yes.'

'So that was why DS Gooch came to pick him up in his car?'

'It must have been. Normally he liked to drive himself, not least because Gooch liked to smoke and he didn't.'

'And you never found a suicide note.'

'No.' She stared at Doug. 'You've done your research haven't you?'

Doug wasn't sure if this was a compliment or not,

but hoped it was the former. 'I'm not an expert, but typically people do leave a note to explain why. Especially if they are leaving a loved one behind.'

'He was very fond of her. In many ways he depended on her. She was his rock.'

'He was fifty-nine I think.'

'You think? You mean, you know.' She stared at him. 'My father had set his sights on retiring at sixty. "I want to reward your mother for putting up with me for all these years," he told me. "Take her on a cruise in the Caribbean. She deserves it – and so much more." That was the last time I saw him. Life got very difficult for me in Exeter, and six weeks later he was dead.'

She fell silent. She rubbed at her eyes, which were moist and red, then suddenly stood up.

'Give me a few minutes will you. I need to sort myself out first. Perhaps you can make us both a mug of tea and there should be some biscuits in the tin with a stag on it.'

Doug switched on the kettle back in the kitchen, found the biscuits, and mused while the water came to the boil. If Danny Duke had been nearing retirement, if he had loved his wife as much as he appeared to have done, then why did he kill himself? And why not even leave a note saying he was sorry? It didn't make sense, Doug told himself, but then if you're suicidal, perhaps sense goes out the window.

When Laura came downstairs – Doug had laid out the tea and biscuits on the main table – she did so at funeral march speed. She was holding a letter in her hand. 'I found this a few weeks ago when I was going through my father's stuff.' She held it in her hand, but didn't hand it over.

Doug frowned. 'I don't understand. He did write a note then?'

'No,' she said, her voice little more than a whisper. 'This was a letter he received just a month before he died.' She still held onto it. 'Can I trust you, Mr Mullen?'

'I hope so,' he said.

'So do I,' she replied.

She put it on the table in front of him and sat down. Doug picked it up and studied the envelope, before slipping the letter out of it. The handwriting was untidy, but just about readable.

Dear Inspector Duke,

You are my last chance. My wife is dead, my daughter is on her own, and I haven't seen her since I was imprisoned.

I didn't kill Layla. God knows that. I saw her on the night she died, but I didn't kill her. I gave her a cigarette. She was scared. I think she wanted to leave Bude.

You've got to believe me. Someone else killed her.

Please, please, please find out who did it.

I was stitched up. I hope to God it wasn't you who did that, because if so, what hope do I have of getting justice. But if it was you, all I can say is I hope that God's righteous anger will descend upon you and you will burn in hell.

Mick Raglan
Prisoner

Doug read the letter twice before looking up. 'Where did you find it?'

'In his study upstairs. What used to be my bedroom, but he took it over when I moved out. Mother never cleared it out. All his stuff is in there, but now that Mum is in a care home, I decided I had to seize the bull by the horns and sort through it all. But when I found the letter, underneath a pile of things in the bottom drawer, I stopped. I didn't know what to do. So I put it back, pretended to myself that I had never seen it and tried to forget it. But then, when you turned up today asking questions, well …'

Doug said nothing. His brain was trying to assess this new information. Danny Duke had received this letter, and presumably never replied or surely Mick would have told him. Of course, Duke had never reopened the case. Instead, eventually, he had killed himself.

'You see,' Laura said, 'I've thought about this a lot. Maybe this letter explains everything. It explains why my father felt so guilty that he killed himself. And it explains why he didn't want to leave a note admitting *why* he was killing himself. Because he didn't want my mother to know that he had got it all so wrong. That way, she could still be proud of him, not ashamed.'

Doug considered this. Her explanation made some sort of sense, and yet there were questions swirling around his brain which demanded answers. When Duke received this thunderbolt of a letter out of the blue, did he, just as Laura had done, stuff the letter away and try to forget about it? Or had he told someone? Not his wife, that was as certain as could be. But what about Gooch? After all, it was he who had been involved in the case too. Indeed, was it possible that Raglan had written to Gooch as well as Duke? Whatever the truth of the matter, there was one big question: how would Gooch have reacted to the possibility that the case might be reopened?

Doug had his theories about Duke's death, but he wasn't sure sharing them with Laura at this stage would be a good idea. What was certain was that the letter from Raglan was important. He just wasn't sure how.

'May I take a photo of it?'

'I'd rather you didn't. I'll look after it, in case it proves to be important.' She held out her hand. Doug paused, then handed it over. He had seen it, that was the important thing. She had trusted him. So now he had to trust her.

'Thank you,' she said. 'What are you going to do now?' Her voice had reverted to the clipped and efficient tone which she had demonstrated in the care home, a manager discussing tactics with one of her staff.

'This changes nothing about my priorities. I need to find out who killed Layla Lark. But I also need to speak to Raglan, if I can.'

'What do you mean?'

'He's dying. He may not have a lot of time left.'

When Doug had told Laura Duke that Raglan might not have a lot of time, he wasn't far wrong. He drove a couple of miles up the road and pulled into a gateway, before getting out and ringing the prison hospital. There was no point in delaying. Inevitably, it took some time to get connected to a staff member who was prepared to tell him anything. When he did get put through to the right place, the Glaswegian accent was a bit of a giveaway. It had to be the hard-nosed woman who had been keeping a beady eye on Raglan the day Doug had visited.

'I was hoping I might be able to have a very brief chat with Mick Raglan.'

'Not much chance of that.'

'You mean he's died?' The news startled Doug. Even though he knew it was bound to happen, somehow it took him by surprise.

'Not yet,' gave the gruff reply. 'He's a tough old bird. But he's on a lot of morphine and spends more time asleep that awake, and even then he's not as chatty – or as rude – as he used to be.'

Doug sighed. What could he really hope to learn from Raglan? Whether Duke had ever replied to his letter? He thought that was unlikely. And yet, suppose he had? The fact was that Doug needed some help. And Raglan's letter, especially the words 'stitched up', chaffed him. He had used them at the same time as appealing to Duke. As if he didn't believe Duke was involved in the stitching up. Now that was something he needed to pursue.

'Nurse, if at any stage Mick is awake and alert enough to speak to me, could you possibly help him to ring me on my mobile. It really is very important.'

'Tell me your number and I'll do my best.'

'God bless you,' Doug said, quite unexpectedly.

'Oh, you're a private eye and a Christian are you?'

'Not really.'

'Me neither. So I don't need your blessing. But I wouldn't object to receiving a box of chocolates the next time you're visiting. Only thing is, it'll need to be sooner, not later.'

What was it he had said to Zoe? *Trust me. I will keep you safe.* Doug stood up suddenly, and hurried to the downstairs toilet, getting there just in time to be sick. He knelt on the floor, in case there should be more. Eventually, he got up, washed his face and stood there, leaning on the basin as he waited for himself to feel better.

'Doug?' It was Becca, in her nightie and with a look of concern on her face. 'Are you OK?'

He shook his head. It was no good pretending.

'You've been sick. I can smell it.'

'Suppose Zoe is dead,' he said.

'What are you talking about. There are lots of possibilities,' she said.

'It's past eleven o'clock. She's not back. She's not answering her telephone. She's either kidnapped or dead.'

'Or she could have hooked up with a guy and is lying in his bed having just had sex. And that, frankly, is more likely.'

'Why is it more likely?'

'Look at what she's gone through in her short life. Imagine it.' She paused. 'Maybe she takes a bit of love wherever she can find it.'

Doug began to cry. He hardly ever cried. And yet

now, when she moved forward and he felt her arms close around him, he howled like an animal in pain. As his body pressed against hers, he was conscious of her bump, her baby, *his* baby, and slowly he calmed down and the tears subsided. Eventually he released himself from her. 'Sorry,' he said.

'Go and have a shower. Then we will sit down and work out what to do. Because feeling sorry for ourselves is not an option.'

He nodded, like a child given a gentle pep talk, and headed for the stairs.

Doug didn't sleep well, even though Becca and he had agreed a plan, namely to contact the police in the morning. 'We don't know much about her, Doug. We don't know what motivates her. Think of the life she has had so far. Maybe she met a guy in a pub and went home with him. She wouldn't be the first. So let's wait and see. Give her time to come back here, and if she doesn't, only then do we contact DI Jennings.'

But despite Becca's calm words, despite the herbal tea she insisted he drank – it was optimistically called Peace – his sleep was disturbed, erratic and anything but peaceful. He tried to close his mind, to wait for oblivion to envelop him, but eventually his bladder forced him out of bed and down to the ground floor toilet. After that he poured himself a glass of water and went over to the window. The sky was clear and a half-moon hung above the town. There was a flash of movement, and then the unmistakeable sound of an owl out hunting. He went to the front door, unlocked it and stood in the shallow porch, hoping for another glimpse. He stood there watching and listening. And that was when he heard it. Not the owl again, but a low sound, muffled and yet insistent. He stepped forward and then saw something that shouldn't have been there – something long and shapeless, half hidden in the shadow.

He knew what it was. He had seen bodies before. By the light of the moon he saw the sheen of her hair, recognised the silver-grey puffer jacket she favoured, and knew immediately who it was. For who else could it be except Zoe? He bent down and touched her, and to his relief she twitched. She was alive.

CHAPTER EIGHT

'HOW IS SHE?' Doug was standing in the doorway of Zoe's room. Becca was sitting half awake and half asleep in the Lloyd Loom chair next to her bed, where she had set up guard ever since Doug had carried Zoe upstairs and lain her down on the bed.

'Still under the influence of whatever it was they gave her, but I think she's OK. She woke up a while back and had a pee. I gave her a bit of water, but she went straight back to sleep.'

'Did you learn anything?'

'No,' she said. 'There will be time for that later. Why don't you make me a mug of tea and a piece of toast.'

'I'm happy to take over from you.'

Becca shook her head. 'We don't know what she's been through. This is nothing personal, but it's best if she sees a female face when she wakes up.'

'Of course,' he said, a fraction too quickly.

'If it was me, then of course I would only want to wake up to your face.'

'Yes.'

'And maybe a kiss too.'

Downstairs he switched on the kettle and put a couple of pieces of bread in the toaster. He went to the front door and unlocked it, and went outside to inspect the spot where Zoe had been left. Maybe there would be some sort of clue – something identifiable

that someone had dropped or a distinctive footprint –
but there wasn't anything like that. He shrugged, and
cast his eyes up and down the pavement (as if some
dodgy stranger might have been lurking!) and then
retreated inside.

He shut the door, and noticed an envelope in the
cage on the back of the door designed to catch the
mail. His first thought was that it was a circular,
except that his name, 'MULLEN', was written on the
front of it in block capitals. The flap was not sealed
down, and he opened it carefully, trying to minimise
his own prints. Inside was a short printed message:
'Shush, or else!'

When Doug had showed the threatening note to
Becca, a short discussion, conducted in whispers
which grew increasingly emotional, had ended with
Becca making her unequivocal ultimatum. 'You're a
dad now,' she continued, patting her bump, 'so stupid
heroics are no longer OK. Zoe was abducted and that
letter was a threat. We can't just ignore it. And you
can't do it all on your own.'

He nodded. He knew there was no point in arguing
with her, and he knew too that she was right.

'Hell, Doug, the police wish we had never turned
up here, but they are the good guys.'

'Not always. For example, based on what Sally
and Laura Duke said yesterday, I definitely don't see
Gooch as a good guy.'

'He's ex-police, Doug.'

'He wasn't when Layla was murdered.'

'We have no option, Doug. Just make the call.'

He made the call, and half an hour later Jennings and Bristow were on the doorstep. Despite his ambivalence about them being there, he was impressed at their prompt arrival. At least they were taking it seriously.

They sat at the kitchen table, from which all the paperwork had finally been tidied out of sight. The only piece of paper was the threatening note which Jennings studied with gloved hands before bagging it.

'So this was pushed through the door last night? And Zoe Finch also returned last night?'

'It was more complicated than her just returning. She was out for the count. Someone must have driven her here. Someone who had kept her isolated and drugged up.' Doug's words were thick with emotion. 'They know who she is.'

'Whoa! Steady, Mr Mullen. There's a lot of assumptions in there. That Zoe was held by some person or persons against her will. That she was drugged by them against her will. That those same persons also issued this threat against you. Before we jump to any conclusions, we need to get the letter analysed by forensics. We can also test her blood for drugs, and we can try and trace her movements during that period when she went missing. I assume she was carrying a phone?'

'She did have a phone, but that has gone missing.'

'You have her number?'

'Yes.'

'Assuming she left the house with it, even if it was taken from her or she lost it, we should be able to get a partial trace on her movements. As for Zoe, can we see her?'

'Just you,' Becca said, taking charge. 'Given what she may have been through, I think it best if your sergeant waits down here with Doug. He can pass on her phone details.'

Jennings nodded and followed her upstairs. Zoe was in bed, sitting up against a plumped pillow, apparently asleep, but when Becca whispered her name, her eyes opened. She looked startled.

'This is Kate, a police detective, Zoe, and she wants to see how you are.'

'You went missing, Zoe. Did anyone hurt you?'

Zoe was silent.

'Did anyone force you to do anything you didn't want to do?'

There was a brief shake of the head. Her eyes were moist.

'You came home here very late last night. Doug found you lying on the ground outside. Did someone drive you here?'

Zoe began to shake. Becca laid a hand on her forearm. 'Don't worry, my dear.' Then she turned to Jennings. 'Another day, I think.'

Outside on the landing, the two women paused before descending.

'Becca, I know you just want to look after her, but she needs checking by a doctor.'

'I'm an accident and emergency nurse with several years of experience.'

'Even so, she may have been raped.'

'One moment.' Becca went into the bedroom she and Doug shared and picked up a see-through freezer bag from the bed. 'This may not be as per your normal procedure, but in here is a sample of her urine, a sample of her blood, and the knickers she was wearing. I used gloves, so there shouldn't be any contamination from me. Hopefully all that will be helpful. Of course, if you want to send a medic round to do a full check-up here, that would be excellent, but I would prefer she was spared the possible trauma of a hospital visit.'

Jennings nodded. 'OK, but there is one thing I want to ask. Neither you nor Doug have told me what her connection to you is. In fact you have been notably avoidant on that score.'

'Off the record?'

'I can't promise that.'

'Well, that is honest at least.' Becca looked at Jennings. She knew she had no real choice. She had to be truthful about Zoe, because if she wasn't and Zoe went missing again, then she would never forgive herself. 'Zoe is Mick Raglan's daughter. She looks very like her mother, Greta Raglan. Naomi Trent changed her hairstyle and colour to try and hide the resemblance, but our concern is that someone has discovered this.'

'So who else knows this except for you and Doug?'

'Naomi, of course. We had to bring her into our confidence. As far as I am aware, no-one else knows.'

'I see. It's a lot to take in.'

'Can I ask if you know Detective Sergeant Gooch.'

'Ex Detective Sergeant Gooch. Yes. I am aware of him. Most people are, one way or another. He's not someone who hides his light under a bushel.'

'Would you trust him?'

'I can't answer that question.'

Becca smiled. 'Well, I guess you not answering it is in itself an answer.'

It was raining, steady and unrelenting from a dark sky, but Doug wasn't going to let that put him off. Becca was staying upstairs with Zoe, so he was the one who had to go out. He didn't care how wet he got. They needed some fruit and eggs and oat milk, so after he had given the dog a quick walk to deal with any calls of nature, he headed for the town. He took a slightly circuitous route, past the Olive Tree cafe, past the Bude Light 2000 and the spot where he had been punched to the ground, and then across the river and past the fateful bus stop. He paused there, sheltering from the rain and hoping for some sort of inspiration to come, but it didn't. Then up the hill towards Sainsbury's he trudged. But before he got there, he found himself passing a bookshop. It looked tempting and inviting, and the rain was coming down harder than ever, so he went in.

Neither Becca nor he had brought anything to read from Oxfordshire, and Becca was going to be tied to the house with Zoe, so he reckoned she might welcome something to lose herself in while Zoe rested. He picked up the first book which caught his eye. He knew nothing much about it except that it had apparently made zillions of pounds, and was clearly in the 'good holiday read category'. He studied the front cover and the back cover and then began to read the first page. A smile spread across his face. This might be fun. And then something made him glance up out of the window. And that was when he saw them. The rain had suddenly eased significantly, but this fact didn't register with him because his attention was totally taken up by the three people chatting on the corner of the side street opposite.

He recognised one of the pair immediately. The wheelchair was a bit of a giveaway: Andy Trent. And the big guy next to him, in bright yellow oilskins, was clearly his brother Frank. Doug's first thought was that this was a great opportunity to go and have another chat with them, but when he realised who the other person was with them, he froze. Despite the long pink waterproof coat and hood, the striking profile of Roxanne Lark was immediately recognisable.

What were they talking about? The centre of Bude is not a big place, so if you go shopping there, bumping into someone you know must be par for the course. Doug tried to tell himself that the likelihood was that this was a casual chance meeting, but he failed to persuade himself. He stood there motionless, the book in his hand forgotten. Roxanne was standing close to both men, and it was as if she had come alive. She bent down to say something to Andy, closer than Doug might have expected if they were just casual acquaintances. Or was it different when one of you is in a wheelchair? He continued to stare, wishing that he could lip-read, in case it might tell him something. But it was clear from the way Roxanne straightened up that the conversation was coming to an end. She said something to Frank, who laughed. Was this just being friends, or something more flirtatious? Both men were smiling. Then Andy raised his hand

175

in farewell and started to wheel himself up the hill. Roxanne gave him a farewell pat on the shoulder, before exchanging a few more words with Frank heading downhill. He stood stock still, watching her go.

'Can I help you, sir?' He turned. A woman in a denim skirt and floral blouse stood in front of him, hands clasped in front of her. 'Sometimes people like a bit of advice when choosing a book.'

'Actually, I'm thinking I might have this one for myself.'

'In that case, a very good choice, sir, if I may say so.'

'But I am also looking for something for my partner.'

'Is this partner a she or a he?'

'A she. She likes things that are a bit more gritty than this.'

'In that case, sir, I am sure I can help you.' And she did.

'Do you spend all your spare time reading in order to keep up with the new books and then offer appropriate advice to people like me?' he asked a couple of minutes later, as he tapped his card.

'I do my best, though I am not so keen on gritty myself.'

'Nor me. I get enough of that in real life.'

She raised her eyebrows, but closed the conversation very gently. 'I hope you both enjoy your books.'

Would Becca really like gritty in the current circumstances? As he resumed his walk towards Sainsbury's, he wondered if he hadn't made a very stupid choice. Maybe he should read the gritty one and let her read the comic crime one. But these thoughts were blown away almost as soon as he had had them. They were replaced by something else. Something that Andy Trent had said about his brother, when he and Becca had gone to his house that first day. What was it precisely? That Frank was a bit soft on Roxanne. Something like that. Had he been talking about the past or the present? Because to judge from what he had just seen, it looked as if it wasn't just Frank who was soft on Roxanne now. And in which case, which one of them did she prefer?

For reasons that he barely understood, Doug decided to make his way back to the cottage via the sea pool. Quite what he was expecting to gain by another visit, he would have found it hard to explain. Indeed it was not a case of him making an explicit decision to go that way, more a case of his feet unconsciously leading him that way. As he made his way up the slope to the headland, he told himself that if he sat there for long enough and tried to imagine himself as a witness all those years ago, then maybe something would occur to him. It was worth a try, he told himself. Anything was worth a try. If the tide was out, he could make his way home over the sand, rather than have to retrace his steps. He stood at the top of the cliffs and stared down at the sea pool. It was grey and cool, and a fine rain was sweeping across the bay. No-one was swimming in the pool. There were a few people walking the beach, and two women surfing in brightly coloured wetsuits, but otherwise it was a day when wise people chose to stay inside.

He stood there for some long time, allowing his brain to go into free-fall, until something made him turn round. Just a few metres away there was a woman in a wheelchair. She was swathed in a yellow kagool, and her eyes were trained on him.

'You're that private eye, aren't you?'

He nodded. 'Doug.'

'Thought so. Don't suppose many people here dig you, Doug?' She laughed.

'I suppose not.'

'I'm Elsie.'

'Nice to meet you, Elsie.'

'Terrible thing, that Layla dying here all that time ago. And now that Josie. I expect you blame yourself, coming here and stirring things up. Sometimes things are best left alone.'

Best left alone? He felt a sudden swirl of anger ripple round him like the wind.

'You think so? That it's best not to ask questions even when a man might have been imprisoned for something he didn't do?'

She held her hand up defensively. 'I'm sure you meant well but …'

'But Josie is dead, and it's all my fault. Is that what you mean?'

'No need to shout.' She spoke very carefully and without emotion, meeting his furious eyes with a steady gaze.

'Sorry,' he said. 'That was completely …'

'Out of order?'

He nodded. 'It's just that …'

'Look, Doug, why don't you buy us both an ice

cream from that kiosk over there, and then I'll tell you something about Mick Raglan.'

'You knew him?'

'I've lived here all my life. Now, ice cream first.'

By the time Doug had returned bearing his offerings of atonement, Elsie had eased herself onto a bench and was looking far out to sea. He slumped down next to her and, like her, stared out across the grey, white flecked expanse of water.

He bit a piece off his chocolate flake and savoured the taste. Despite the circumstances, he was suddenly engulfed by the memories that eating a 99 often brought back, of times spent at the seaside when all had been well with his world, before his father had walked out on them, and before his mother's mental health had disintegrated.

'So what do you want to ask me?' Elsie said, breaking into his memories.

'What do you want to tell me? Most people here don't want to answer my questions, so why don't I shut up and just listen. I'm right at the end of my tether, so if you have something to say, I'm all ears.'

She sighed and took another lick of her ice cream. 'Mick was alright. Liked a beer, but then they all did. Rugby lads they were. Him and Andy and Frank Trent.'

'Was Jim Gooch part of that group?'

'Goochie? Oh yes.' A smile spread across her face. 'He was a fine figure of a man in his rugby kit. He was a bit older than them of course, mostly involved in the training. I used to watch them all when I didn't have anything better to do. Lots of us did, checking out the talent. Of course I was in a wheelchair even then, so it was all wishful thinking. Who wants to take on someone like me?'

'And was Gooch still part of the scene after he joined the police?'

'I think he was based up in Exeter after his training, but he'd still come back and help out when he could. I believe he'd inherited his parents' house by then, so I expect he rented it out to holidaymakers. Of course, he was part of the investigation team when Layla died. I guess his local knowledge was viewed as a bit of an advantage. Detective Inspector Duke was fairly local too, but he didn't know the town like Goochie.'

'What about Andy Trent?'

She looked across at him, her eyes sharp as razors, and then she burst into laughter. 'You mean because we're both in wheelchairs? You think it makes us bosom buddies?'

'No, no!' Doug could feel his face reddening.

'I think you doth protest too much.'

'Honestly, I just want to find out more about him.'

'Liar!' She smiled. 'Anyway, we do meet up over a coffee sometimes, and discuss accessibility issues in the town, and generally have a chinwag. He's OK, a bit loud, but good company. We would never be buddies though.'

'Did you ever see him with Layla?'

This time she didn't laugh, didn't even crack a smile. 'You suspect Andy?'

'No. Don't go spreading that rumour. Look, his daughter was one of Layla's best friends, and you have got to know him. I'm an investigator which means I ask endless questions in the hope that one or two of the answers will eventually help me get to the truth. And sometimes those questions may be close to the bone. So whatever you do, I ask you not to talk to anyone about this conversation. And don't quote me as suspecting Andy or indeed anyone else. The fact is that Josie is dead and Naomi is in hospital. That is quite enough.'

'Point taken.'

'So did you ever see Andy and Layla together?'

She pointed what was left of her ice cream at Doug. 'What you've got to remember is that I wouldn't have recognised Layla then. She was just one of a horde of schoolgirls with short skirts. It was only after her death, when photos of her popped up all over the media, that I realised who she was. You see, I had seen her a couple of weeks earlier. I was doing a circuit on the marsh, and she was there chatting to Andy and his brother Frank, and there was that lanky guy, Matt I think his name is. Anyway she was flaunting herself and they were like bees around a honeypot.'

'Flaunting herself? What do mean exactly?'

'Maybe that's a bit harsh, me being a sour middle-aged woman spilling out her own regrets. Her clothing was perfectly ordinary and sensible: jeans and a pink waterproof jacket. Nothing obvious. But she was chatting away and tossing her blonde hair, and they were all hanging on her every word. Or that was how it seemed to me. You're playing a dangerous game, I thought, with those testosterone-filled men. And it turned out she was.'

'And you told the police?'

'No. Why would I have? It wasn't evidence of anything. On the night Layla died, I was in hospital having another blooming operation, and it was only weeks later, after a period of convalescence in Truro, that I got back to Bude. By then Mick had been arrested and charged.'

'Can you tell me anything about Frank?'

'Well he was part of the rugby drinking group for a few years. But then he joined the merchant navy and was gone for ages. I think it was the Christmas before Layla's death he turned up at a party at the rugby club. After that he settled down back in Bude. Odd-jobbing for people. He came and installed a new worktop in my kitchen a couple of years ago. He had some stories to tell.'

'Girlfriend stories?'

'Tall tales of the sea. I didn't believe half of them. Quite a sad person if you ask me. But then it takes one to know one.'

'Do you think Naomi knows something that she's not telling us?' Doug said.

On his arrival back at the cottage, he had made a cup of tea and given Becca a pastry which he had picked up from a bakers he had spotted.

Becca didn't respond. Or rather she did, but she didn't answer the question.

'This is good,' she said, taking a bite out of her pastry. 'I love lemon curd.'

They were sitting on a bench in the small garden at the back of the house. Zoe was upstairs asleep, and this was as far away as they dared go. Doug had even double-locked the front door so that Zoe could in no way slip out while their backs were – literally – turned. Rex was sitting expectantly at Becca's feet, waiting for crumbs to be dropped.

'You haven't answered my question,' Doug said quietly.

'Everyone has secrets. That's how we survive, by keeping some things to ourselves because we daren't share them with anyone else.'

'Are you talking about yourself? Are you saying there are things you don't want to share with me?'

She looked at him, her eyes as sharp as pencils. 'It's not all about you, Doug.'

'Even so …'

'Even so, let's stick with Naomi. Yes, I think she knows things that she is scared to talk about. She thought she would be safe with us, but she wasn't. Maybe being with us put her in increased danger, because someone thought that she was more likely to spill the beans to us.'

'So the stone throwing …'

'So the stone throwing was an attempt to either scare us off or to scare her into keeping quiet. The fact that she rather than you got hit by one of the stones was pure chance. But the question now is if she recovers, is she likely to finally tell us any secrets? But there is another, more important question. If she recovers, if she wakes up and she is able to talk, how long will it be before she, like Josie, plunges unobserved off a cliff, and you get blamed again?'

Becca took another bite of her lemon curd pastry. Doug nibbled at his own *pain au chocolat* without really tasting it, because her comment had kick-started a sudden thought inside his confused brain. 'Why didn't they do that with Layla?'

Becca frowned. 'What?'

'Why didn't the killer push Layla off a cliff? Much easier to do that than kill her in the sea pool. Much safer too.'

Becca sipped at her tea while she considered this. 'Because it wasn't preplanned?'

'I reckon so. A chance meeting, followed by an act of passion. A meeting which turned nasty, terrible things said, threats made. Who knows what? But something happened which was enough to drive the killer over the edge.'

'Remember Layla was only fifteen.'

'Don't fifteen-year-olds have sharp tongues? All children try to manipulate their parents, from the moment they cry and discover that that is the way to get more milk. From what we've learned, I suspect Layla had become rather good at manipulating adults, especially boys and men. But on this occasion she met her match.'

'Doug, I hope you are not implying that she got what she deserved?'

'No. Of course not. I … I …'

'You said she met her match.'

'What I meant was that she didn't anticipate how the killer might react to her behaviour. As you say, she was fifteen, increasingly aware of her sexual power, yet maybe rather naive …'

Becca's phone rang, bringing the suddenly awkward conversation to halt.

It was a short conversation. 'Yes … yes … of course.' When it was over, she looked across at Doug, a frown on her face.

'Naomi is awake, sort of. Eyes open. Not speaking.'

'Can we go and see her?'

'We can't both go and leave Zoe on her own.'

'Well, if I go and turn on the charm, at least we can reassure her we are looking out for her.'

Becca leaned forward and, with sudden tenderness, kissed him on the lips.

'You, Doug, may be the last person she wants to see.' Becca's words were as softly spoken as she could manage, but she knew they would hurt. 'I was thinking maybe I should go in on my own.' She paused for the briefest of moments. 'If that is alright with you?'

He didn't say anything at first. He understood the wisdom of Becca going to try and see Naomi on her own, but that didn't mean he was happy. It brought back an old and odd memory – him standing on the periphery of the end-of-term school disco because the only girl he really fancied was dancing with someone else. He had felt excluded then, and the child in him felt excluded now, insisting that this was his investigation and he should always be in the thick of it and asking the questions. Of course, the adult in him recognised that the situation was more complicated than that, and that he was being a spoilt kid, but that didn't stop him from feeling those things.

'Doug,' Becca said again, but with a distinct edge. 'Is that alright with you?'

He nodded, and only then looked at her. 'Becca,' he said, 'I came back from town via the sea pool and I also bumped into a woman in a wheelchair who knew quite a bit about the Trents and Gooch and this all got me thinking.'

'Thinking what?'

'That maybe I've got it wrong about Layla's murder. I mean, what if Layla's murder was both by chance and deliberate?'

'That sound a bit … weird, Doug.'

'I mean, we've assumed that the meeting must have been by chance, and that the killing an act of passion rather than a cold-blooded murder. Because it makes no sense for a killer in their right mind to choose that sea pool as a place to kill someone. There are many easier and safer places to commit murder and get away with it. But let's suppose that the killer saw Layla and Mick chatting at the bus stop and saw too that Josie Archer had observed it. Maybe the killer was even with Josie at the time. The killer then follows Layla out to the sea pool and kills her there. Because he realised that this was his perfect opportunity. Not only has he – supposing it is a he – shut Layla up for good, but he has lined up Mick as perfect fall guy.'

'So the motivation was what?'

'It might still have been an act of passion – a guy tries to have sex with her and she resists, maybe even taunts his manhood. But I am inclined to think it was something else, that Layla was a danger in some way to the killer. She knew something and so she had to die.'

* * *

Sometimes the best laid plans come to naught. Becca was feeling rather nervous when she arrived at the hospital. It was Patience, the nurse whom she had chatted up and persuaded to keep her informed, who had rung her and tipped her off about Naomi regaining consciousness. But when she asked for her, it was to discover that she had finished her shift some quarter of an hour earlier.

When she then asked if it was possible to see Naomi Trent, the answer was a firm no. 'Family only.'

'I'm a friend. She was staying with us when the incident happened,' she pleaded. 'If I could just see her, I'll keep it very short.'

The nurse frowned, not at her, but at someone behind her. Becca turned round.

'What are you doing here?' Judy Trent said. She was flanked by Joshua. There was no sign of Andy.

'Naomi has been staying with us. She was walking with us when she was hit by a rock. I am naturally very concerned. I'm a nurse and I wanted to see if she was alright.'

'It's family only,' Joshua said, stepping forward.

'When she was scared, she chose to come to us,' Becca said. She had no intention of giving way to his bullying. But in the circumstances, her words were risky, and Judy, for all her smaller stature, was not easily intimidated either.

'I am her mother,' she snapped. 'I will look after her when she is allowed out of the hospital. She will come home and we will all make sure she comes to no further harm.'

'I understand,' Becca said, cursing herself silently.

'In that case,' Joshua said, 'you had better clear off. Not just out of here, but out of Bude altogether. Do you get my drift?'

Becca knew from her experience working in a hospital that she had no power in this situation. Family always trumps everyone else. But she wasn't going to cave in to a bully who had already attacked Doug. She eyeballed him. 'You think Doug and I are the problem here. But you're wrong. The problem is that someone has killed Josie and someone has damned nearly killed Naomi. That isn't Mick Raglan or either of us. It's someone local, very likely from Bude. Maybe the killer is someone you know. Do you get *my* drift, Joshua?' And with that she turned and left.

'A bit soft on Roxanne.' While Becca had been out on her ill-fated hospital visit, the words had been playing hopscotch inside Doug's cranium. So too had the scene he had witnessed from the bookshop – Roxanne and the two Trent brothers and her discreet pat on Andy's shoulder and Frank's laughter. What were her feelings for each of them and theirs for her?

And by the time Becca had returned with her face glum, he had made the decision that he would go and pay Roxanne a visit. Not in a public space as the Olive Tree had been, and not in their holiday house, but in her own home where there would just be him and her. And he had a simple plan in place to achieve it.

'Bad news,' Becca said after they had kissed. 'The family won't let me near her. Warned me off in fact in no uncertain manner. Her mother is more formidable that she looks. And Joshua is protective and aggressive. I can't say I'm surprised. Anyone fancy a cuppa?' she said.

Zoe – she was watching a programme about buying a new house and gaining a wonderful new life in some sun-kissed foreign country – didn't even register that she had heard the question.

Doug shook his head. 'I thought I'd go and return Roxanne's medical kit.'

'There's no rush is there? I've not had a chance to replace what I used.'

'I'll sort that out with her.'

'I promised to replace the things I used.' She spoke emphatically. She expected him to give way. But he merely shrugged and pulled on his anorak, zipping it up decisively.

Becca stared at him and frowned. He looked back at her. He could read the frown. *What are you not telling me, Doug?*

'Oh, I nearly forgot,' he continued. 'When I was in town earlier, I bought you something to read from the bookshop. A choice of two books, actually. The woman there was very helpful.'

'Was she indeed?' Another frown. Was this a flicker of jealousy? A case of *I'll get it out of you later, Doug?*

'Anyway, I'll be off,' he said. 'I won't be long.' And he opened the front door before any inquisition could develop.

When he got to Roxanne's house, there was a considerable pause before she opened the door. 'Oh!' she said. There was surprise and – if Doug's antennae were operating accurately – also disappointment wrapped up in that word.

'I've brought this back.' He held the first aid box out in front of him as if it was a box of chocolates for a would-be girlfriend.

'Thank you.'

'Can I come in?' he said quickly, metaphorically getting his size ten foot in the door. 'I really need to speak to you, as a matter of urgency.'

She hesitated. 'You could have rung first.'

He pressed on. 'I really won't take up much of your time.'

She conceded, though not very gracefully. 'You'd better come in.'

'I'm not sure Becca has managed to replenish the items she used, but I've left a tenner inside so you aren't out of pocket.'

'There was no need.'

'Even so.'

'Would you like a tea or coffee?'

'No, but thank you. Shall we sit down?'

She sat down on the middle of the sofa and he sat on a matching armchair. They were clean and without any worn patches or stains as far as he could tell. New and nice quality too. He admired them and asked where she got from.

'Online,' was the reply. Doug's eyes flicked around for signs of another visitor, but if there had been someone in the house when he knocked, she had made a good job of clearing away any give-away signs. And her visitor was either hiding upstairs or they had slipped out of the back door.

'I presume you didn't come here to ask me about my furniture.'

'No. Actually, I wanted to ask you where you were on the night of Layla's death.'

There was a short, but distinct silence. The question had clearly taken her by surprise. It would have been a surprise to him if it had not. She looked down at her hands, as if she had just noticed some imperfection – a broken or scratched fingernail or a hitherto unseen wart.

'That was a long time ago.'

'Are you saying you can't remember where you were the night you daughter died?' Now that he was here with her, Doug wanted answers, and he had no intention of pussy-footing around.

'I'd like you to go.'

'Why won't you answer my question? I'm on your side. I am trying to establish the truth.'

'The police discovered the truth. It was Mick Raglan.'

Doug raised his hands to his head and took two deep breaths. It was as if, ever since he had arrived in Bude, he had been battering his head against brick walls, and none of them had shown any sign of giving way.

'I said I'd like you to go,' Roxanne said. 'And not come back.' She was on edge, pleading rather than demanding.

Doug had had enough too, but he wasn't ready to give up or to high tail it out of Bude. 'Mick Raglan is on his deathbed and he is insisting that he didn't do it. At first I wasn't convinced about him, but the more

I've looked at the case and the more I've spoken to people and heard their lies and evasions, the more I've become convinced that he is telling the truth. Layla's killer is out there, and he is local, and almost certainly it is he who killed Josie Archer too.'

'Josie fell. Or jumped. I read it in the paper.'

'Roxanne, Josie was pushed. Murdered because she knew something.'

'How can you possibly know that?'

'There were two sets of footprints in the area from where she fell. Of all three options, murder is the one which makes most sense.'

'None of it makes sense.' She was on the brink of emotional collapse.

He waited for her breathing to subside, then leaned forward. 'Roxanne. I know this is difficult, but I am going to ask some more questions. You can say "no comment" if you want, and I'll move on to the next one and the next one and so on. And if all you want to say is "no comment", then I'll go back to my holiday cottage and in the morning I'll pack the car and leave Bude. And then you will have to live with whatever happens after that.' Doug knew he was being manipulative. He was also lying because he sure as hell was not giving up, not yet. But in the circumstances he felt being manipulative was a very minor sin.

'So question number one is this. When precisely was it that you first realised that Layla was missing.'

Roxanne shuddered. Doug waited. Was this how it was going to end? Everyone, even Layla's mother, uncooperative, their heads buried in the sand. He began to count to ten silently. He had got to eight when she suddenly spoke.

'I … I … never did notice. I assumed she was upstairs in her bed. I didn't know she wasn't there until the police came the next morning and told me that she was dead. I mean her school coat and jacket were strewn around here as usual. She had obviously been in the fridge. There were the remains of a pizza on the table. So nothing unusual.'

'You didn't go and check her room?'

'She was fifteen. She didn't allow me in, not even to clean it up.' And with that, the floodgates opened. Suddenly there was no stopping the outpouring of her grief and guilt. 'You probably think I was bad parent, not knowing where she was, not checking her whereabouts, but I really did try to be a good one. I gave her space. I trusted her. My parents had watched me like a hawk in my teenage years and I ended up hating them for it. I couldn't leave home soon enough. I didn't want Layla to do that. So I gave her freedom to make her own choices.' She paused. 'And sometimes she made mistakes. But that's how they learn isn't it?'

Doug nodded, silenced by the sadness of what he was hearing. But she hadn't finished.

'What you don't expect, what I never even dreamed of, was that one morning the police would come knocking on my door to tell me my daughter was dead.' She broke down then, totally, sobbing and sobbing. Doug got up and passed her a box of tissues from the dresser, but he felt helpless to comfort her. Instead he waited until she indicated that she was ready to continue.

'I can't imagine what it must feel like,' he began. 'But if I succeed in finding out for certain who it was who murdered your daughter – whether it was indeed Mick Raglan, or whether it was someone else – then I hope that will be of some comfort to you.'

'Comfort?' She looked at him as if he was a lunatic.

'Not comfort exactly,' he said, backtracking quickly. 'That was the wrong word. What people nowadays call closure.' Closure wasn't just a word to him. He had felt closure over the death of his friend Ben, but he wasn't going to go into that now. But the fact was that he was now able to live with himself and with the memories. That was all. When he remembered Ben, he still felt the guilt.

Roxanne continued to stare at him with her large eyes. Doug moved on.

'Do you have any idea where your daughter was going that night? Did she say anything about who she was meeting?'

'No, she didn't. It was a Friday night. A time to let down her hair. Meet up with her mates. Have a drink in someone's house or on the beach or go to a house party if someone's parents were away.'

'You must have asked Josie and Naomi if they had seen her.'

'Naomi said she hadn't seen her since the end of school. Josie told me she did see her at the end of school, but Layla had been rather cagey about her plans for the evening. Anyway Josie went home and didn't see her until much later when she spotted her talking to Mick Raglan.'

Doug grunted. 'None of the reports I've read said

anything about whether Josie went and spoke to her then.'

'That's because she didn't. I asked her that same question.'

Doug fell silent as he tried to put what he had heard into some sort of order. There was a lot to think about. If those three had been such best friends, how come on a Friday night neither Naomi and Josie went out to party or drink with their bestie Layla? And how come when Josie did see Layla at the bus stop, and saw her cadging a smoke off Raglan, that she never went over to her. Isn't that what you might expect her to have done? Gone over and joined in, if only to cadge a cigarette for herself. Something about it all smelt a bit fishy.

Doug decided to move on, into what was potentially even more dangerous waters. 'From what you've said, I assume you were with someone on the night of Layla's death?'

He paused, but Roxanne didn't respond. Her eyes were cast down, unwilling to look at her inquisitor. 'I know this may be difficult, but I hope you feel able to tell me who that was. At the very least, if you were, then it would rule that person out. And let me underline that all this information will remain strictly between you and me – unless of course it becomes essential information in a trial.'

'You promise?'

'Yes.'

Time passed. Roxanne was breathing increasingly hard and fast. Doug wondered if he might have to do something. His brain tried to locate the information it contained about hyperventilation, but it wasn't something Doug had ever needed to draw on in the real world. *Don't do the paper bag trick! That's old hat.* He remembered that from some first aid course. Do keep them calm. Becca would know best. He would ring her if he needed to.

'Frank Trent,' Roxanne said suddenly into the silence. Her voice was soft, only just audible.

Doug tried not to show his surprise. 'Roxanne, I need more information than that. Times and place.'

'I went out about eight o'clock. I drove to a house in Hawthorn Avenue. Frank was already there. He let me in. He was cooking a chicken and wine dish. It smelt lovely. Tasted good too. He used to work in the kitchen at a hotel out of town. But this was his night off and—'

'So I assume this wasn't his house.'

'It belonged to one of his friends. The friend was out of town and allowed him to use it as long as he left the place clean and tidy, and paid for the laundry.'

'I need a name, Roxanne.'

She shut her eyes tight. Doug could almost see her counting to ten while she summoned up the courage. 'Gooch,' she said, so softly that Doug wondered if he had misheard. 'Detective Sergeant Jim Gooch.'

'I see.' It was the sort of thing Doug was inclined to say when he really didn't see, when he couldn't work out all the angles and implications.

'Remember you promised to keep this private.'

'I remember,' he said, and immediately moved on. 'I presume you had supper, and then stayed on for a while with Frank. When did you go home?'

'Two o'clock.'

'And when you got home, you went to bed without checking if Layla was in her room?'

'Yes.'

'And what about Frank?'

'What about him?'

'Was he still at Gooch's house when you left?'

'Yes. Gooch wasn't due back until the morning, but Frank said he was going to tidy things up and then head for home. He had a flat in the hotel where he worked.'

'So why didn't you meet there?'

'Because it was small, just one room, and no cooking facilities beyond a microwave. Whereas Gooch's place was smart and clean and comfortable. Frank wanted to impress me.'

'Thank you for trusting me.'

'If it wasn't Mick, who could possibly have wanted to kill my Layla? She was a bit wild, but lots of kids are at that age. The hormones are going doolally. What does anyone expect?'

Doug wasn't sure what people expected. But the statistics were clear, that murders were often committed by people who were known to their victim. He knew that, and he suspected Roxanne might be aware of it too, but in the circumstances he felt it best not to mention it. Because if Layla knew her killer, then the chances were that Roxanne would have known them too.

'I'll go in a minute, but I do have one or two more questions, if that's OK. Do you have any idea what Gooch was doing out of town that night?'

'Seeing a woman, I expect.'

'Any idea who?'

'Just someone out of town as I recall.'

'Like Camelford?'

She looked puzzled.

'Like anywhere, I guess.'

'And was this rendezvous of yours with Frank a one off or …' He never finished the sentence. He just let it hang in the air, waiting for Roxanne to respond. And wait he had to do. He was just wondering if she would ever say something when she sprang to her feet. 'Three times and never since. Now would you please go!'

Doug stood up and thanked her. 'I will indeed go.' He pulled on his coat and went to the door, which she was holding open. Just as he was passing, she grabbed his sleeve. 'Whoever it was, it wasn't Frank. He would never have done that to Layla – or to me.'

'I've had an interesting chat,' Doug said on his return. Zoe and Becca were sitting watching the TV. 'But I need a pee before I tell you about it.'

Zoe got up. 'I'll make you both a tea. Then I want to tell you both more about yesterday.'

A few minutes later, they were sitting down at the kitchen table. Zoe had produced some chocolate biscuits and laid them out on a plate in a fan shape. She seemed distinctly on edge.

'When you're ready, Zoe.' Becca had devoured a biscuit in very short order.

'You're not to say anything until I've finished. Nor do I want you to judge me. I just want you to know what happened. I am who I am.'

Doug wondered what was coming. Although Zoe had apparently waited for his return, it was as if she was barely conscious of his presence. She was facing Becca and her words seemed to be directed solely at her. He felt like an observer, irrelevant. Then he had a sudden realisation. It was Becca whose acceptance Zoe wanted. It was as if Becca, in her mid-thirties, had been adopted by Zoe as her mother. A mother who would listen in silence, forgive whatever she had done, and then tell her that everything would be alright. He sat still, not daring to bite into his biscuit for fear of breaking the spell.

'I just wanted to get out of the house. I thought if I went out on my own rather than tagging along with you, no-one would connect me with any of this. So I walked, right along the coast, all the way to Widemouth Bay. It was amazing. The wind in my hair, sea birds squealing above me. When I got to the beach, I took my boots and socks off and went for a paddle. It's ridiculous, I know, but I imagined that maybe I had paddled there before. I wondered if my dad had carried me on his shoulders out into the waves. It felt like he must have done. Then I realised I was hungry, so I went into the cafe and bought myself some food and then an ice cream. There was this guy watching me. Nice looking, curly hair, and so I thought what the hell, and I went over to him and asked if he had a car and could give me a lift back to Bude.'

She took a breath, and then a sip of her tea. 'Stupid of me, you'll be thinking, but I reckoned I could look after myself and as it was he did take me back to Bude, and then asked if I wanted to have a drink, and I thought why not. So we went to some pub and we had a drink and then another drink and then, God, I suddenly felt really woozy. He said he'd take me home, but I guess he meant his home because the next thing I remember is I was lying in a bed with no jeans or pants on. The curtains hadn't been drawn and it was dark outside. I could hear noises in the bathroom. He was singing in the shower. Can you believe that? Anyway, I got my clothes and boots back on, tiptoed downstairs, and let myself out. My phone was flat, but I had this crazy idea that if I walked for long enough I'd find somewhere that I recognised and then I'd be able to get back here. And I did. But of course I didn't have a house key and I was so sleepy that I just lay down in the front garden. So that's it. I don't want to answer any questions. What I want to do now is go and have a nice long soak in a warm bath.'

She padded off up the stairs, and Doug and Becca waited in silence until they heard the bathroom door shut and the rattle of the pipes as the taps were turned on.

'Date rape?'

'Date rape.'

'At least she's not dead.'

'I'll ring Jennings and update her.'

Jennings had given Doug her work mobile and he got through almost immediately. He explained the situation. 'Have you got the results of her bloods?'

'We haven't. It's too soon.'

'It looks like date rape to us.'

'We'll be checking for that. I'll give them a nudge in the ribs. How is she in herself? Do you think we're looking at a prosecution here? I presume she would be able to identify the man.'

'I can't speak for her. Anyway, what's the chance of a successful prosecution if she does want to proceed with one?'

'That's a tricky conversation to have over the phone. If you like, I can get a female officer to come round and talk to her. Unless you think your Becca might have a better chance of gauging how she feels. As regards our current investigation, it may not be relevant. From what you've said it sounds like a random hook up, but it could be that this guy was deliberately following and watching her. In which case, if we can get an ID, we can hopefully haul him in. Are you with me?'

'Yes.'

'Anyway, I'll keep you informed. Bye.'

'Bye,' he said, though his mind was elsewhere. He would have put this down ninety-five per cent as a random pick-up, except for one thing: the threatening letter in the letter box. But if Zoe walked home as she said, did that mean the rapist – call him what he was, he told himself – had followed her all the way just to threaten her? It didn't seem likely. And yet the threat – *Shush, or else!* – could as easily be a message to Zoe as a message to himself.

'Are you going out for a walk?' Zoe said.

Doug was standing in the porch, the door half open. They had eaten, and it was eight o'clock, dark but dry, the moon adding a pale light to that of the streets lamps that were working. 'I'll never sleep,' she added.

'We'll go together. All of us. Safety in numbers.'

'Thank you. I feel such a fool.'

'Don't beat yourself up. Stuff happens.' He smiled. 'Anyway, let's see if Becca is up for a stroll. Don't tell her, but I really don't want to leave her alone at home.'

Back inside, Becca agreed as long as they didn't go too far. 'I'm knackered. And this baby is having a game of football in my stomach. Give me a hand with my trainers will you, Doug.'

And it was while he was on his hands and knees that he had a eureka! moment. He finished tying the bow on Becca's right-hand trainer and stood up. Zoe was coming downstairs with a pair of white trainers in her hand. They looked spotless, new even. He didn't want to alarm anyone, so he said nothing beyond, 'I'll get my shoes on now.'

He went over to the shoe rack. His were there in their rightful places: trainers and walking boots. Of course he recognised Becca's three pairs of assorted footwear. Which left one pair unaccounted for, a pair of black trainers. They were the ones that he had removed from Zoe while Becca had been giving her a medical once-over. And they were muddy, clearly unwashed. He said nothing. He had a vision of the man getting the drugged Zoe onto his bed. He had taken off jeans and pants, but before that he would have had to remove her shoes first, because there was no way that he could have removed those jeans otherwise. He had a terrible glimpse of how it might have been, the man tugging violently at the trainers, cursing the mud maybe, then yanking the jeans down, tearing at her pants, and then … He picked up his own trainers, as nonchalantly as he could and laced them on. There it was, the evidence he needed, Zoe's filthy trainers. And whoever the guy was, whether relevant or not to the investigation, Doug wanted to know. And he wanted the guy to know that he knew.

'Sorry, I forgot to do my teeth.' Zoe began to walk back up the stairs, moving rather gingerly. Stiffness from the previous day, Doug decided.

He finished tying his laces and went over to Becca. He whispered. 'Her black trainers. The guy must have pulled them off. There's bound to be DNA on them.'

She cut across him. 'Doug, she doesn't want to.'

'What?'

'She doesn't want to pursue the guy, even if she were to see him in Bude. She doesn't want the police involved.'

'But—'

'But nothing,' Becca said, her whisper rising to something much sharper. 'She doesn't want it. She feels like a fool, she feels despoiled, and the last thing she wants is the police getting involved. She just wants to forget the whole thing.'

'But—'

'That's her right, Doug.'

Doug felt frustration swirling around inside him. Her trainers had seemed like a gift. He wanted to argue about it, but knew there was no point. Then something else occurred to him.

'But Becca, suppose he didn't use a condom? What if she ends up pregnant?'

'She won't. I gave her the morning after pill.'

'You what? I mean how did you—'

'She had some in her handbag. We decided it was a case of better safe than sorry.'

Doug stared at her in bemusement, as he tried to process this new information.

Her eyes were unflinching as she stared back at him. 'Don't judge her, Doug. If you were female, you would know that one can never be too careful. Anyway, you'd better text DI Jennings and let her know how the land lies and that we don't want a bright-eyed uniformed officer knocking on the door tomorrow morning.'

There was a distinct atmosphere as the three of them, plus Rex, headed towards town – over the canal, along the Crescent, over the Neet, and then along the Strand. However the atmosphere was mostly inside Doug's head. Becca and Zoe walked hand in hand, and talked trivialities, mostly clothes and make-up, anything to avoid talking or thinking about what had happened in the last twenty-four hours. Doug was silent, walking a pace or two behind them, the dog walking obediently to heel. He kept glancing left and right, alert to the possibility that they could be being observed. Nothing was quite working out he told himself morosely, and when push came to shove he was no nearer finding Layla's killer than when he had first arrived in Bude. In short he was feeling very sorry for himself. His ribs were still giving him grief, and absolutely no-one (and that included Zoe) was cooperating with him. He might as well pack his bags and leave.

He had reached this point of misery when the two chattering women in front of him came to a sudden halt and Doug almost collided with them. For a moment he wasn't aware what was going on. And then he realised they were both looking at the Pirate pub, and Zoe had raised her left hand and was pointing across the road at it. Becca turned and put a finger up to her mouth. Doug stayed silent. There was no need to ask questions. This was the pub the guy had brought her. The acronym 'CCTV' flashed across his brain. Surely they would have some. The police could access it, see who the bastard was, and maybe see if anyone else was involved.

'Let's keep going,' he said, 'past the bus stop and then left over the little bridge and head for home.' No-one argued. They had all had enough for one day. The only problem was that the day hadn't had its fill of them yet, because at that moment four figures came out of the pub: first Andy Trent in his wheelchair, then Frank, then Matt and finally Gooch.

'Come on, Doug.' Becca's words were softly spoken, but urgent. Doug heard them, but he wasn't going to take her advice, not this time. He had had enough of Bude, and whatever happened he wasn't going to back down. He faced them, arms hanging loosely at his side, like Gary Cooper about to take on a whole bunch of bad guys. Rex, taking the part of Cooper's naive partner, stood alert and still, sensing the tension in the air. There was just the road in between.

'I'm surprised you still dare to show your face around this town, Doug.' Gooch had pushed his way in front of the others, asserting his authority.

'I'm surprised that you do,' Doug replied, stepping forward himself. 'After all you were one of the officers who sent an innocent man to prison for the murder of Layla Lark.'

'How dare you spread lies like that. Mick Raglan was convicted by a jury of twelve good men and women.'

'Mick Raglan was framed.'

'Only you think that, Doug.'

'I think that too.' Becca's voice rang across the darkness.

'It's best to stay out of things that don't concern you, darling. And best if you all pack your bags and leave. Otherwise there's no knowing what the good people of Bude might, in their righteous anger, decide to do.'

'Let's go,' Becca said, pulling at Doug's coat. He glanced at her, and saw fear in her face. But that, and Gooch's dismissive 'darling', only served to drive his anger up another notch.

Doug lifted his hand and pointed directly at Gooch. 'Who killed Layla Lark? Who killed Josie Archer? And what is the truth behind Danny Duke's death? If you answer those questions to my satisfaction, I will happily head for home and never return.'

The three of them turned away and continued along the river.

'What the heck were you playing at, Doug?' Becca hissed. 'You'll only make things worse.'

'I wanted to spread some dissension in their ranks and get them scared.'

'Well you've made me scared.'

'At least one of them is a killer. But maybe the others aren't aware of it. We need to flush the rats out. We need to force them to make a mistake.'

They walked on, turning left across Nanny Moore's footbridge. Zoe had let go of Becca's arm and was a short distance behind the two of them, fiddling with her phone. Doug stopped, waiting for her to catch up. 'Zoe,' he said softly. 'I don't want to hang around here. I've been attacked here once before. Let's get back to the house and then you can check out your messages.'

'No messages.' She held up her phone so that he could see the screen. 'I got a video of some of that. Not the beginning, but I reckon it might be worth showing to your police inspector. Especially the blatant threat.'

CHAPTER NINE

THEY MET IN a lay-by, the same one where they had rendezvoused a couple of times previously, when secrecy and privacy had been an issue – as it was now. There was no-one else around. It was early and no-one had pulled up for a pee. There was no lorry driver taking a power nap after a long drive down to the south-west. They stood opposite each other, a wary distance between them.

'Are you alright?' she said. Somewhere deep inside she still had a soft spot for him.

'Why shouldn't I be.'

'You've been like a bear with a sore head ever since Mullen arrived in Bude.'

'He's like a pig in search of truffles. Sooner or later he'll find something.'

'But there's nothing to find, Mick Raglan did it. End of story.'

'Mullen doesn't think so.'

She stared at him, looking hard into his eyes. 'But why are you on edge? I know you didn't kill the girl because you were shagging me at the time.'

He grunted. 'Danny and I put Mick Raglan away. It was our finest hour. And now a jumped-up private eye is doing his damnedest to undo all of that.'

'Suppose he is right?'

'He isn't. Anyway, evidence is what he needs. No-one will take any notice of him if he can't come up with evidence, and he's not going to find any of that.'

'What about Josie Archer?'

'What about her? She fell or jumped. What does it matter which.'

It was at that moment that a white van came bouncing unsteadily into the lay-by. Its driver jumped out and rushed towards the hedge.

'Did you hold a gun to Danny Duke's head?'

He looked at her, his eyes as black as coal.

'That's what Mullen thinks,' she continued.

'I don't care what Mullen thinks.'

I always liked Danny,' she said. 'God only knows why I got taken in by you.'

The van driver emerged from the hedge and headed back to his van, lighting up a cigarette as he did so.

'I guess that's my cue to leave.' She walked to her car, got in, and drove off with a squeal of wheels.

Breakfast was interrupted by the arrival of DI Jennings. She accepted a coffee, but without enthusiasm. Her priority was to see Zoe's video, which she watched three times without comment. Then she sat upright and looked at Doug. 'What did you mean by "the truth about Danny Duke's death"?'

'I visited Danny's wife Sarah. She's in a care home with dementia. Not much help, except that she clearly hates Gooch. I've also spoken to his daughter Laura. She has been clearing out the family home. She found a letter which Mick Raglan had sent to Danny a few weeks before his death.'

'Have you got it?'

'No, she let me read it, but refused to let me keep it.

'And?'

'In it Raglan insisted he was innocent. He admitted he saw Layla, and claimed that she seemed scared. He thought she wanted to get away from Bude. He said that he had been stitched up, and that if it was Duke who had done that, then he hoped God's righteous anger would fall upon him and he would burn in hell.'

'Righteous anger?' Jennings's antennae sprang to attention. 'That was the expression that Gooch used in the video. Are you sure you are remembering it correctly?'

He nodded. 'Laura wouldn't let me photograph it, but I scribbled it down as best I could afterwards. Those words "righteous anger" struck me at the time. Maybe Mick had got God while he was in prison.'

'But from what I've heard about Gooch, he doesn't seem like a religious type.'

'No. I've been thinking about it. Maybe Duke showed him Raglan's letter. Or …' he paused. 'Or maybe Raglan sent Gooch an identical a letter. Maybe Gooch still has it, maybe he's read it again recently and those words are embedded in his subconsciousness.'

Jennings frowned. 'That is possible. Very possible.'

Doug felt relieved that she was taking his theory seriously. He had feared she would poo-poo it, or see it as an irrelevance to the main case. He leaned forward and tapped on the table. 'So my thinking is that Raglan felt that either Duke or Gooch had stitched him up.'

'Maybe, but what Raglan thought gets us nowhere. The bigger question is, did either of them kill Layla, or did one of them plant evidence to secure a conviction? If the latter, then who on earth did kill her?'

Doug shrugged. He had his theories, but he wasn't sure they were strong enough to share with Jennings.

Jennings was studying him over her mug of coffee. 'Doug, you've done enough digging around, upsetting people. So my guess is that you have your suspicions.'

'But nothing more than suspicions.'

'Humour me.'

'Andy and Frank Trent, Matt Tomkin, and of course Gooch.'

'Why them?'

'They were all great mates at the rugby club. They still hang out together now.' Doug paused, briefly wondering if he should say what was on the tip of his tongue.

Jennings seemed to notice this hesitation. She said, with studied casualness: 'No-one else?'

He sighed. He had to say it. 'Andy's son, Joshua, was very keen on Layla shortly before she died. So don't rule him out.'

'Keen on Layla? Can you be more … precise?'

'Sexually active.'

'And who told you that?'

'I'd rather not say.'

'Doug, this is serious. I would be entitled to take you to the station and give you a formal interview if I were to believe that you are withholding important information. So I will ask you again: who told you that?'

Doug glanced at Becca and Zoe, then turned back to Jennings. 'Naomi Trent.'

'Ah.'

'She's not going to admit it to you police, not if it risks putting her brother in prison. Anyway her mother Judy and the rest of them will claim she's not well enough to be interviewed at present. They will claim you're harassing an ill woman.'

'But she told you, so if we had to, we could call upon you to testify. Under oath.'

'That's your call. I merely want to discover the truth.'

'But you've no firm evidence, Doug. And given that Andy is in a wheelchair, he couldn't have killed Josie.'

'But one of the others could have. Friends stick together.'

'And blood is thicker than water.'

Doug shrugged. 'Maybe. But families often fall out.'

She got up. 'I'd better be off. But please don't disappear in case I need to talk to you again.'

'That's a sudden change from being told to clear off back to Oxfordshire.' Doug followed her out, shutting the door behind himself. 'What about the pub CCTV?'

'We are onto that already.'

'Zoe won't testify against the guy.'

'But if we can identify him, and maybe see if anyone else was hanging around with him and Zoe, then who knows where that will lead.'

'I'm going to find Gooch and speak to him.'

'Speak to him?'

'Yes, speak to him, ask some questions and make sure I get some answers.'

'I strongly advise you to think very carefully about that. Beating the shit out of him won't help. You'll end up in custody, and then no-one will believe anything you say about Layla's murder. They'll say you've got a grudge. Do you understand?'

'Sure. I understand, Inspector. I have a plan, and it involves lots of witnesses.'

'Be very careful,' she said.

'Can I ask you something? You've had a chance to study all the paperwork of Raglan's trial. Obviously Raglan saw Layla on the night of her murder. That is irrefutable. He admits it. But as regards the murder, that is just circumstantial evidence. There must have been something more solid than that.'

'Something very solid – a bracelet. A bracelet belonging to Mick Raglan was found in the sea pool.'

'And DI Duke and DS Gooch were the investigating officers that day.'

'It was their case.'

'That wasn't exactly what I asked.'

Jennings shrugged. 'I can't say more than that. I was learning my trade in the Met in those days.'

'Even so, it is something you might want to think about.'

When the call came, it took Doug completely by surprise. Neither he nor his phone recognised the number, but then calls from strange numbers were nothing new. When this job was over – as it would be one day, sooner or later – he would need more work to follow, so he didn't think twice about responding.

'Is that Mr Mullen?' The Glaswegian voice was a giveaway.

'Yes it is.'

'I've got Mick Raglan here. You wanted to speak to him. But try to keep the conversation to the point. He is very poorly.'

'Hello, Mick. This is Doug.'

There was a grunt, followed by a cough and then a thin wispy voice. 'Hello. How is my daughter?'

'Zoe is fine,' he lied. 'She is staying with us in Bude.'

'Is she being a good girl?'

Doug ducked the question by asking one of his own, the one he had to ask. 'I need to ask you something, Mick.'

'OK.'

By this point in the conversation, Doug had made his way out of the house, and was heading along the pavement away from town. More importantly away from Zoe.

'What is it?' Raglan rasped.

'I want to know why you lied to your daughter.'

'What do you mean?'

'Was it because you were afraid that if you told her the truth, she would walk out of your room and never come back?'

There was a strangled noise down the line, and then the not so dulcet Glaswegian tones of his nurse took over. 'I don't know what you said, but you've blooming well upset him.'

'I don't care if he is upset. Hold the phone so he can hear this question.' Doug paused briefly, before taking the plunge. 'Mick, how long did you and Judy Trent have an affair?'

There were various muffled sounds. Doug waited. Then called out, 'What did he say?'

More sounds. Then the brusque sound of his nurse again. 'Three weeks, he says. That's all, three weeks.'

'He wrote a letter to Danny Duke from prison. Did he ever get a reply? Ask him that.'

More mumbling. 'He shook his head. No.'

'Does he know what happened to his bracelet? It had the letters MR on it.'

'That's the end of the conversation,' she said. 'Any more questions, and you'll be talking to a corpse.' And with that the call was terminated.

Jennings sat at her makeshift desk and scratched idly at the nape of her neck. Doug Mullen had got her rattled. When she had first encountered him, she had decided he was just trouble. Trouble certainly seemed to have been following him ever since he had arrived in Bude. Then she thought he was maybe just a guy who thought he knew it all – and didn't. And now she thought … Hell, she didn't know what to think. She needed to focus, reduce things to their essence.

Fact number 1: Doug was a private eye being paid by a convicted murderer to investigate the murder he had been convicted of – and more than ten years after the event.

Fact number 2: since Doug had started asking questions, he had been attacked, and he and his companions had been pelted with stones with such ferocity that one of them had ended up unconscious in hospital.

Fact number 3: one of his companions, Zoe, may

have been date raped. (Memo to self: where the hell are the forensic results on the bloods, and how long is it going to take to check out the CCTV from the Pirate?) So, not currently a fact, but if the bloods and CCTV points in that direction, the perpetrator needs to be arrested and charged. The question then would be: is the rape relevant to the wider investigation?

Fact number 4: Doug came across as being a lot sharper than many of the colleagues she had worked with over the years. (Memo to self: do not underestimate Becca Baines!)

Fact number 5: if someone were to pump her full of an infallible truth drug, she was almost certain that she would be saying some pretty complimentary things about Doug's theories.

So what now?

She was still considering this question when an email pinged into her inbox. She read it once quickly, and then with much greater care. Doug was right. Zoe's bloodstream had contained Rohypnol, the date-rape drug. She rang Bristow immediately. He had taken up residence in the office of the Pirate, so that he could get the assistance of the manager if and when it came to identifying anyone of interest on the CCTV.

Bristow didn't answer. She cursed and texted him, then sent him an email for good measure, both with the same message. *How much longer? Blood results in.*

She stood up, stretched and went and inspected a small box on the table where kettle, mugs and other essentials were laid out. She took a donut – chocolate icing with coloured sprinkles – and sank her teeth into it.

Her mind, however, was elsewhere. What was the last thing that Doug had said, when she had confirmed to him that Duke and Gooch were the investigating officers? 'That wasn't exactly what I asked.' She thought about this, rolling it around in her mind as she absent-mindedly devoured the rest of the donut. Then she picked up another one and took a bite out of that too.

'Everything all right, ma'am?' Liam Protheroe was studying her, as were Chas and Rhona Fernie. That was probably because she had a reputation for eating super-healthy, organic weird stuff, and definitely not two donuts on the trot.

She pulled out her wallet and placed two tenners on the table. 'Someone go and stock up on the food and drink. I've got things to do.'

It wasn't long – Protheroe had drawn the short straw and had not yet reappeared with nice things to devour – before Jennings was on her feet again, pacing around and asking if anyone knew a Sergeant Alan Creighton.

'Can't say I do,' Fernie said.

'He was part of the original investigation. I need to speak to him. Urgently!'

'In that case,' Chas said, 'give me a few minutes. I reckon I could track him down for you.' And less than fifteen minutes later he had not only located him, but magicked him up on the other end of a video call. 'Sorry for the delay, ma'am,' Chas said. He seemed to mean it, but Jennings was super impressed. 'He's in Spain. Got some sort of security job out there. Not sure what happened, but rumour is he left under some sort of cloud, so best not to comment on that fact.'

Jennings ignored the stupidity of the advice. Did Chas really take her for an idiot, and why on earth would she bring it up anyway? She decided that Chas was one of those intelligent guys who can also be remarkably daft.

'Alan,' she said breezily after introducing herself. 'So sorry to interrupt your day, but I think you might be able to help me out on one or two points of detail about the Layla Lark case. Do you remember it?'

'Course I do. It was all over the news. I played a small part in the investigation.'

'But a key part, so I am told.' She could butter people up with the best of them. 'Which is why I am contacting you, in the hope you can help me. I'm just reviewing the case.'

'I'll try to. It's some time ago, but the old brain cells are still pretty active.' He tapped his head and laughed. Jennings did her best to laugh back.

'I was wondering if you can just talk me through what you remember of those first couple of hours after the body had been found.'

'Well, I was looking forward to the end of my shift. It must have been sometime after 6 a.m. when the call came in, and then myself and Jack Ingram were high tailing it down to Bude. When we got there, we found a couple of dog walkers waiting by the sea pool, and we saw her body floating in it. Of course, we didn't know who she was, and neither of the dog walkers could help on that score. Mind you she was face down in the water, so no surprise really. She was clearly dead. We knew we must not touch her, even though it felt wrong, if you know what I mean, to leave her floating there. But I was a pro and I knew my job. We secured the scene, took the details of the two witnesses, and waited for reinforcements to arrive. The pathologist was first, and the crime scene jonnies and the detectives of course.' He paused and smiled across the video link. 'How am I doing?'

'You're doing very well, Alan. Can you remember the names of the detectives?'

'Course I can. I'm not senile, not yet.' Creighton despatched another smile from Spain to Cornwall. 'The head honchos on the case were DI Danny Duke and DS Gooch.' He frowned. 'Not sure what Gooch's first name was. Everyone seemed to call him Goochie or Sergeant.'

'And they turned up together at what time?'

'Time? Soon afterwards. Maybe seven. Is it important? It is a long time ago and I did have other duties to perform, not just clock people in and out.' He laughed yet again. Jennings wanted to scream, but resisted the urge.

'Of course you did, Alan. This review is not about you, don't worry. So to clarify, the two of them arrived together and …'

'No.' Creighton held up a hand as if his true metier was traffic control in the days when traffic lights were few and far between.

'Not Duke. He didn't come until later. Gooch was the first detective on the scene, as well as some spotty DC. To be honest I can't remember his name right now. It'll probably come to me in the middle of the night. But don't worry. If it does, I promise I'll wait until morning before I ring you with the info. Cub's honour!'

This time Jennings failed to match his grin. 'So when did Duke arrive?'

'Not before I went off duty. Mind you, he was there bright and early the next day. They both were. The crime scene guys hadn't finished their sweep on the pool.'

'Thank you, that has been most helpful. If I have any more questions, I hope you don't mind if I contact you again?'

'Any time, ma'am. I am always glad to help His Majesty's boys in blue – and girls of course.' And he raised a hand in mock salute.

Jennings smiled through gritted teeth and waved back. 'Thank you, Alan,' she said, while hoping against hope that she never came across him again.

'Another donut, ma'am?' Protheroe had returned. 'To go with your chai latte.' He placed a cup on the table.

'Thank you, Liam, I'll take a rain check on the donut.'

'Of course, ma'am.' Young and polite. She liked that.

The sugar hit was making her feel a little queasy – not that she would ever have admitted it. She took a sip of the chai and returned her attention to the computer. She began to flick through the records again until she found what she wanted – an inventory of everything that had been found in and near the sea pool. The key piece of evidence was Raglan's bracelet. It was ordinary enough, plain silver with nothing else to distinguish it except the letters MR. Standing for Mick Raglan, although Jennings wondered if there was a joke hidden in there, MR for Mister. If she remembered correctly, his wife Greta had given it to him, after she had got pregnant. A cute way of thanking him for his sperm. Had they needed IVF? The thought jumped up from nowhere and lodged itself in her head. Not that it mattered, although it would have mattered at the time to them. It had certainly mattered to herself.

She shook these musings away and focused on the inventory. A number of things had been found on the bottom of the pool – coins, three odd earrings, a long screw – as well as plastic rubbish floating on the surface. But overall, not much. They must have had someone who kept it pretty clean. They would want to prevent injuries to bare feet, which meant that anything they did find in the pool that day was likely to have been recent. She looked up. Rhona Fernie was standing by the food and drinks table and looking bored. She beckoned her over and instructed her to check out the cleaning regime for the sea pool in those days. Fernie seemed puzzled by the request, so Jennings explained her reasoning in words of one syllable and dismissed her with a flea in her ear.

What now? She needed to speak to Doug Mullen. She rang his mobile. No reply. She rang Becca Baines. She answered immediately. No she didn't know why he hadn't answered, but he had gone out. Maybe he had got his phone on silent.

Jennings dropped her voice. 'Is your house guest with you?'

'Upstairs.'

'Good. So here is the situation. The bloods which you extracted from your guest do indeed contain significant traces of Rohypnol. We are still going through the CCTV, but no further news beyond that. But whatever you do, don't let her out on her own. Is that clear?'

'Crystal.'

'Do you have any idea where Doug is?'

'He's gone off in the car. Maybe he's looking for Gooch.'

'I told him not to.'

'Why don't you just pull Gooch in and take him off the streets for a couple of days?'

'Evidence. It was over fifteen years ago.'

'Josie was only a few days ago.'

'I'm as frustrated as you are.'

There was a prolonged silence. Jennings could hear heavy breathing down the phoneline and it reminded her that Becca Baines was pregnant.

'How is the baby?' she said suddenly. She remembered her own pregnancy, and how vulnerable and yet how fierce that had made her feel.

'Baby is fine.'

'Boy or girl?'

'I'm not letting on. Even to Doug.'

'I could put a uniformed officer outside your house, if you like.'

'That won't be necessary.'

'I thought it might make you feel safer.'

'The arrest of Josie's killer will make me feel safer.'

'Of course. I understand that.' There was another

silence, briefer this time. 'Can you please make sure Doug rings me soonest.'

'Yes,' Becca said. The call was over.

Doug was fed up with asking questions and getting evasive answers, fed up with working for a man who lied to his daughter to save face, and fed up with waiting for the police to get their act together. Once he was clear of Bude and on the Atlantic Road, he jammed the accelerator hard down and headed south-west. The car was Becca's. His own trusty Ford had been totalled a few weeks previously, though fortunately not when he was in it. He liked the fact that it was red, even though that was never a colour he would have chosen for himself. But now, with his driver's side window open and the clouds scudding across the sky in front of him, he was a naughty schoolboy skipping lessons, a teenager hitting the open road, and a man on a mission.

He was fed up with waiting for things to happen. That was giving them the advantage, letting them set the agenda. Exactly who 'they' were was not a question he could currently answer. Of course he had ideas and theories but that was not the same thing as evidence. It was evidence he needed. He had muted his phone. Stupid at one level and yet he needed to be unhindered in his thinking, without distraction.

It took him just twenty-two minutes to arrive at his destination. Here and there he had taken some risks with his speed, but he didn't have time to waste. He got out of the car, jogged the short distance to the front door and pressed the bell twice. The door opened a few seconds later.

'You!'

'Me!' He gave her his broadest smile.

'What do you want?' She was not pleased to see him.

'Are you going to invite me in for a coffee?'

'No.'

'Got company have you?'

'I'm about to go out. Shopping.'

'Ah, the good old "shopping" excuse.'

She pursed her lips. 'What exactly do you want?'

'Ten o'clock tonight. At the Storm Tower in Bude.' She stared at him, perplexed as hell – or so he hoped. 'I'm ready to strike a deal. To make it all go away.'

She laughed then, the sort of braying sound that he would have expected from her. 'Who on earth do you think you are?'

Doug stared back at her. She knew. Maybe not everything. But plenty. Her words told him so. She hadn't said 'to make what go away?', but 'who on earth do you think you are?'. She had had a friendship with Gooch for long enough, very likely a sexual relationship with him.

'I know about the letters.'

'What letters?'

'That Raglan sent to Gooch and to Duke.'

There was a flicker of uncertainty in her eyes, but she remained silent. Did she know about them, or was that news to her? Not that it mattered. What mattered was that he had thrown her off balance.

'I've had enough,' he continued. 'I can't prove anything. But I have connections with the police, and I can pass all my information onto people who will take it very, very seriously. Or I can destroy it and forget it if someone makes it worth my while. So, it's cash. Five thousand. To cover the fee that Raglan won't now be paying me.'

Her face hardened. *I am not a woman to be trifled with*, the face said. But then he had no interest in trifling with her.

'Pass the message on,' he said. 'If it doesn't happen tonight, then the deal is off.'

A hint of a smile crossed her red lips, but it was not a comforting one. 'You're walking a tightrope, Mr Mullen.'

'My friends call me Blondin!' He grinned back like a lunatic, which pretty much reflected his mood. He walked back to the car, got in, and did his best impression of a driver with a car which did 0 to 60 m.p.h. in three seconds. It wasn't a particularly good best impression, but when he swung the car into a 180-degree turn at the end of the cul-de-sac, the wheels of Becca's car squealed very satisfactorily. He hit the brakes, and glanced across at Candice Kipling. She was standing in the doorway, motionless. He gave her a regal wave, and jammed his right foot down on the accelerator again.

The die was cast and the Rubicon crossed, wherever the Rubicon was. He'd look it up when he got home. He'd also have to confess to Becca that he had been maltreating her car a tiny bit. But that was for later.

Just a mile away he pulled up at a convenient service station, filled up with fuel, and then rang Jennings.

'I need your help,' he said.

'What's going on, Doug?' She sounded wary, but

the fact that she was calling him Doug seemed a good sign.

'I have a plan,' he said. 'I'm not going tell you the details. But there is one thing you can do for me.'

'I hope you aren't going to ask me to do something I will later regret.'

'So do I.'

The Pirate was only a short walk from their temporary operations base, and Jennings was there in double quick time. Bristow was sitting in a tiny office that smelt of beer and stale cigarette smoke. He was looking very pleased with himself. 'Sit yourself down, ma'am.' He cleared an empty sandwich container from the chair next to him, and edged his chair to the right.

'This here is the lady in question—'

'The victim.'

'The victim, ma'am. And this here is the man she arrived in the pub with.'

'The subject.'

'The subject, ma'am.'

'When did they arrive?'

'Well over an hour prior to this, ma'am.'

'That's enough ma'ams, Chris. But I will need precise times in your final report.'

Bristow lifted up a sheet of lined paper. 'All the times are down here.'

'Have you been able to identify the subject?'

'No. Seems like he was a holidaymaker. Rob, the publican, says he's only seen him two or three times, and not at all after this particular evening. Maybe his holiday let had run out and he went home, or maybe he got cold feet and the next morning decided to make himself scarce.'

Jennings made no comment on Bristow's theories, though both seemed reasonable. It fitted in with Zoe's description of their getting together at Widemouth Beach.

'How many drinks has she had by this point?'

'Only three. But if it is OK by you, perhaps I can just take us back to the beginning and then highlight all the key moments that I have established.'

Jennings nodded her approval. She was still quietly wary of Bristow after his careless talk to Gooch, and yet she was also impressed by him. Not that she was going to tell him so, at least not until he had proved himself doubly.

'Here we are back at the beginning. At 5.47 they sit down here. He has a pint of beer and she a cider. I've checked my own assessments of the drinks with Rob, and so I feel confident that they are accurate. At 6.20 they each have a new drink, his another pint, hers a gin and tonic. At 6.44 she leaves the table, I presume to go to the Ladies, and returns at 6.49. Now this is where it gets interesting. During this period while she is absent, at 6.46, someone approaches the young man at the table. Can't get an ID on him because we only get a back view, but they chat for fifty-five seconds and then, watch very carefully.'

Jennings watched. Bristow had slowed the speed of the video down. 'Coming up now.' The man who had approached the table and chatted to the subject had put something small down on the table and, after the briefest of delays, the young man slipped his hand out and picked up the item.'

'Is that a pill?'

'I've studied it very carefully, and although it will need to be properly analysed by an expert, it looks like it to me. Almost immediately the victim returns and drains her drink. The subject gets up and presumably goes to the Gents. He returns about two minutes later, drains his drink, and disappears again, presumably for two more drinks. I'll fast-forward, but this takes over eight minutes. Rob told me it wasn't too busy, so I do wonder why it took him so long. The victim seems to be able to see him, and at one point waves her hands in frustration, but then if you watch she seems to lose sight of him because she looks around the pub until suddenly he appears again and places two fresh drinks on the table.'

They watched silently while this all took place, Bristow slowing and fast-forwarding with confidence. 'There, look, ma'am.'

Jennings watched it all unfold, saw what Bristow had described about the victim's behaviour, and saw, at the end of it, the victim take a pull on her drink. Another fast-forward some five minutes, and the victim was draining her drink and then slumping back in her seat. The subject by contrast has barely touched his latest drink. He left his drink unfinished, and shortly afterwards was supporting her up from the table and away out of sight.

'So,' Bristow concluded, 'it looks like the Rohypnol was put in her drink by the subject away from the table after the subject had bought that last round of drinks.'

'It looks like it. But it is not going to stand up in court on its own. The *defence* would argue that anyone else in the pub might have done it. As for what we assume was a Rohypnol pill, the defence would doubtless say that it was impossible to prove. Maybe it was something the subject bought for himself – some pep pill to improve his performance or even a sweet.'

'Yes.' Bristow's disappointment was obvious, and Jennings registered this.

'But whatever the court may think, I'm convinced, Chris. This is where and when she was drugged. The question is can we identify the subject. Get Rob in here now.'

Less than a minute later Bristow was back with the publican. Jennings gave him her best ingratiating smile. 'So sorry to bother you, Rob, but we need to know who this guy is? I know the visuals aren't great, but maybe you can at least give us a list of anyone who you know for certain was in that night, between 5.30 and seven.'

'That's quite an ask. One night merges into another.'

'OK, think back to this young man we are interested in.' She turned to Bristow, who quickly reversed the video to where the subject stood up to go and order more drinks, the point when his face was closest to the camera. 'He came up and ordered three rounds of drinks. Do you remember anyone who spoke to him then or was propping up the bar nearby?'

Rob shook his head.

'You must remember something. This was only a few days ago.'

'My brain doesn't work like that. Sorry.' And with

that, he left the room, shutting the door behind him with a bang.

'My brain doesn't work like that! He's taking the piss. Shall I go and drag him back?'

'No!'

'No? Why ever not?'

'I'm going to storm out. You take a few minutes to pack up your stuff, then go out and make a point of thanking Rob for his cooperation. Buy yourself a beer. If Gooch or any of the Trents or that waste of space Matt is there, make a point of acknowledging them if they seem interested in you.'

'I don't understand. What's the point of all this?'

'I haven't finished yet, Sergeant,' she hissed. 'Just listen to what I say and then make sure you do it.'

And so she explained, he listened, and at the end of it, she smiled.

'I'm relying on you. Don't let me down. Now I'm going to storm out. See you later.'

The garage door was open. Doug got out of the car and approached it warily, as if it might be booby trapped. There was no-one there, but a number of cardboard boxes, some filled, indicated that a clear-out was in progress. He hovered on the edge, taking in the beams that stretched from one side to the other. It was impossible for him not to imagine the body of Danny Duke hanging there.

'Oh my God, you gave me a start!' Laura Duke had appeared in the doorway between the garage and the main house. She was wearing a white T-shirt and denim dungarees, but remarkably both appeared to be spotless. Her right hand was on her upper chest, in a stereotypical gesture of surprise. But then stereotypes do reflect reality, albeit sometimes a simplified version.

'I should have called out,' Doug said.

'I hate this garage. I'd tear it down tomorrow if I could.'

'I understand.'

'I thought you were the man with a van. He's promised to take away everything in here. I don't care what he does with the stuff, just as long as he takes it. Then I can lock the garage up and pretend it doesn't exist.'

'Yes,' Doug said, not sure what else he could say.

'Come through into the kitchen. I can't talk here.'

Doug followed her, shutting the inner door behind him.

She switched on the kettle and dug out some mugs. 'I don't know how Mother stood it. Maybe she couldn't. Maybe that's what pushed her over the edge into dementia. I don't know what the medics would think of that as a theory, but it makes sense to me. Imagine living so close to where your husband killed himself. Why the hell couldn't he have gone and done it somewhere else? Well away from here. Jumped off a cliff maybe. There are plenty of them in Cornwall. Tea?' she asked switching with a suddenness which alarmed Doug. 'That's all I've got here. I think the milk is OK.'

A woman on the edge. Those were the thoughts which jumped into Doug's head, but they were not the words which splurged out of his mouth. 'Maybe because someone held a gun to his head.' Doug had told himself that he would approach the subject carefully. *Not like a bull in a china shop.* Those had been Becca's words, hackneyed but wise. But here he was, doing exactly the opposite, rushing in where angels fear to tread.

Laura let out a piercing scream. Then, 'Shit!' She slammed the kettle down and shook her left hand. 'Ow! Ow! Ow!'

'Under the cold tap!' Doug ordered. He knew what do to with scalds, just as he knew what to do with lots of minor and indeed major injuries. You don't live with an A and E nurse and not pick up a lot of useful tips.

Laura had gone into freeze mode. Doug took this as his cue to switch on the cold tap, grab her hand, and thrust it under the running water. She was mewing, though whether this was just physical pain or something more Doug wasn't sure. 'This will help,' he said, as if she couldn't have worked this out for herself.

A few minutes later they were sitting at the table, each with a mug of tea which Doug had finished making. There was a bowl of overripe bananas, one of which he handed to her and another which he ate.

Laura looked at the banana as if she had never seen one before, and then at him as if he was a strange species too. 'You said …'

'I'm sorry. I didn't mean to. Well I did, that's partly why I'm here. But the words just jumped out.'

'You said someone held a gun to my father's head.'

'I said maybe. It's a theory. I can't prove it.'

'But that letter I found from Raglan. I've read it several times. It makes sense of what happened. My father received it and felt guilty that he had put an innocent man in prison. And when my mother was away, he got so low that he killed himself.'

'Perhaps, but there is one thing it does not make sense of.' Doug took a sip of his tea in the hope that she would follow suit and that – old wives' tale or not – it was the panacea to all ills. 'Do you remember what you said a few moments ago? "Why did my father not go and kill himself somewhere else?". That's the key question. If he loved your mother, as I think he did, surely he wouldn't have done it here in the garage. Would he really have wanted her to find his body hanging in the garage on her return?'

'But if he was so depressed as to want to kill himself, would he have thought of that?'

Possibly not, Doug told himself, but he had no interest in acknowledging that to her. 'And there is another, practical question. There must be easier ways of doing it than hanging yourself. As you said, why not just go and jump off a cliff somewhere?'

Laura rubbed at her eyes. They were red and moist. 'So what's your theory?'

'He needed to tell someone about the letter. He couldn't tell your mother, so he told Gooch, the only man he could safely tell. I think your father wanted to take the matter further. I think he told Gooch that he was going to do that, and I think Gooch gave him an option. Hang himself, or get a bullet in the head.'

Laura was silent for several seconds as she processed

all this. 'Are you saying Gooch killed Layla and then my father?'

'It's possible. Gooch was involved in some way. But I don't know if he was the killer.'

'How can you prove it?'

'I really don't know.' Doug put his head in his hands. Ultimately only Gooch knew. And maybe … maybe he had got it all wrong. Maybe Danny Duke had fallen into a deep depression that night and reached the point of no return. So he had gone down to the garage on his own volition and killed himself.

Then something extraordinary happened. Laura stretched her undamaged hand across the table and, just as he had done earlier to her, grabbed him by the wrist, digging her fingers so hard that Doug yelped in pain.

'Sorry!' she said, without sounding it. 'Tell me, is there any way that I can help nail the bastard?'

CHAPTER TEN

IT WAS 6 p.m. when Bristow made his way through to the bar. Rob looked up. 'All done?'

'Just thought I'd have quick one before I head for home. Candlelit dinner and the works awaits me.'

'Birthday?'

'Anniversary.'

'How many now?'

'I've lost track.' He laughed. 'But she will know. Cheers!'

Rob wiped the bar with a small towel, but without enthusiasm. He looked up at Bristow. 'Not sure your boss likes me.'

Bristow glanced around. The pub was sparsely occupied, and no-one very near. Even so, he spoke softly. 'She's just very frustrated. This date-rape case isn't going anywhere. They are hard to pin down at the best of times.' He leaned forward confidentially. 'And we aren't getting anywhere with the Josie Archer death either. That idiot of a private eye insists that it was murder, but – and this is just between you and me – there's no evidence for that and I reckon it will all get closed down soon enough.'

'And Layla Lark? He stirred up a lot of fuss about her death.'

'Only because he's being paid by Raglan. Quite apart from his fee, he's got two weeks free in a holiday house. I reckon when that's run out, he'll cut and run. He's that sort of guy. In it for the money.'

He drained his beer. He had had enough. He had done what Jennings had told him to do, said what she had told him to say. The bit about his anniversary was his own embellishment, but it was true. Twenty-nine years. But the romantic candlelit meal was going to have to wait. Time to ring her and make his apologies. She would understand. The job comes first. And he did have a present for her, hidden in his sock drawer at home. He wanted to show her he loved her, because after all those years, he still did. He hoped she felt the same about him.

It was a goodish night for the meet up, Doug decided. Certainly not cloudless, but there were patches of clear sky for the half-moon to shine through and provide some light. He strode along Breakwater Road, the canal on his right and the dog happily scampering along on his left. There was enough artificial lighting here, but once he had reached the far end and started to clamber up behind the holiday houses, it became a place of uneven paths and dark shadows. He stumbled, almost falling over, and as he righted himself one of the dark shadows moved a couple of paces forwards.

The guy was tall and he had a baseball bat in his right hand. 'There's been a change of plan.'

'But it's my plan.'

'Not any more. We've changed it.'

'Who's we?'

'Give me your mobile phone.'

'I left it at home.'

'I don't believe you.'

'I didn't want it to be stolen or smashed up by the likes of you.'

'Don't get funny with me, or it'll be your woman that gets smashed. The fat one. Now turn round, arms in the air, while I search you. You piss me off or resist, and it'll be her that pays the price. Are you with me?'

Doug turned round and lifted his hands high. He was seething, but he knew he had to keep calm. He reckoned that if he got the baseball bat off the guy, he'd be able to get the better of him, but that would not serve the overall plan. The guy patted him down. Rex growled, a low, threatening 'hands off my boss' growl.

'Why on earth bring a dog like that with you? He couldn't scare a kitten.'

'He needed a walk. I don't want him doing a poo in the house.'

'Well you'll have to leave him here.'

'He stays with me. He'll get lost. He doesn't know the area. I don't want him falling off the cliff like poor Josie Archer.'

The man hesitated, thrown off balance by this unexpected development. Or maybe he had a soft spot for dogs.

'He's a Westiepoodle,' Doug ploughed on. 'I rescued him from a burning house. His owner died, so I took him on. They are white usually, but he's black.'

'I can see he's black. I'm not blind.'

'He won't be any trouble. Anyway if I let him off the lead, he'll just follow us wherever we go, so frankly there's not much use—'

'All right, all right. You can bring him. But if he so much as squeaks, we'll dump him out the window of the van.'

'God bless you, sir.'

Doug could feel the man's eyes glaring from behind his mask. *God bless you, sir?* He realised that he was in danger of pushing his luck. 'So what *is* the new plan?'

'You follow me to a van. You get in the van. You keep your mouth shut. Is that clear?'

'Absolutely.'

The van was parked in Breakwater Road. Doug realised he must have walked past it. It was white and unobtrusive, just one of many thousands – tens of thousands probably – of unmarked white vans in the country. The windows were tinted. Not so typical of a white van, but very effective in hiding its occupants from prying eyes.

The man opened the passenger door and Doug got in.

The man got in the other side. Doug had put the seatbelt on. The man grunted. 'Hands.' Doug held them out, and on went the cuffs. Then a cotton bag down over his head. 'Any noise and the dog gets it.'

Doug should have been scared, but somehow he wasn't. It wasn't going to plan, but he had known that it probably wouldn't. This was predictable.

The dog had already jumped up onto his lap, and he held him there, stroking him gently. He tried to judge from the movements of the vehicle where they were going. On the coast road south-west he thought, past their cottage and up the hill, but judging the distance travelled was difficult, and in any case it was not as if he knew the area well, and even if he had, he doubted that that would have been of much use to him. What he needed was to keep his wits about him when they did finally stop, and hope for the best.

The van was moving faster now, rolling from side to side, bumping over a sudden hump in the road. 'Running late?' Doug said, and got the predictable response to shut up or else. Then suddenly the vehicle swerved right, and Stirling Moss rammed his brakes on.

Doug felt Rex stiffen, and he resumed his stroking. A car went past them, hooting as it did.

'Bitch!' the man said.

'Everything alright?' Doug said. He could sense the tension in the man. He was breathing heavily. Whoever he was, reacting calmly to sudden or unexpected events was not one of his strengths.

'Thought we were being followed. Thought you were setting me up, but it was some bitch in a VW convertible who thinks she owns the road. She even had the nerve to give me a V-sign as she was passing.'

'Women, they think they own the world these days.'

'Shut it.'

Doug shut it. He tried instead to listen to the sounds outside. Given the road they had driven along and the time they had been driving – five or six minutes he reckoned – when the guy pulled off the road and came to a halt, Doug's guess was they had pulled into the car park that looks down on Widemouth Bay. He had been there one day with Becca and Rex. No trees. The only cover was low, so once you were down amongst it, you would be hard to spot, but if you got to your feet and ran, you would be fully exposed. Of course, this was nighttime, but as he had noted when he had left the house, there were plenty of clear patches of sky through which the moon could shed its light.

Laura Duke waited. The adrenalin rush of chasing the van and giving two fingers to its driver had subsided, but the sense of excitement was still high. This was what she had missed. As a kid she had been addicted to surfing and climbing. Later she had abseiled and sky-dived for charity. And then it had all fizzled out. The desperate attempts to have a child had overtaken everything else until Jack had left her for a younger model – how pathetically stereotypical that was – and after that her parents had taken centre stage.

But now the adrenalin was mixed with anger. If DS Gooch had really held a gun to her father's head, she wanted to be in at the kill – as it were. She wanted him in court and then in prison. She wanted him to pay, above all for the misery that her mother had gone through.

She pulled into the front drive of one of the many holiday houses not inhabited at this time of year. From here, she was able to observe with the aid of a telescope – her dad had loved bird-watching – what was going on. The van was still there, but if that was meant to be the new rendezvous place, how come no-one else had arrived? Her mobile beeped, indicating another incoming message. It was Becca: *What is happening?*

Laura rang her. Easier to do that than ping endless messages back and forth.

Becca answered immediately. She was clearly worried. Laura explained, trying to keep her calm, but without success. 'Look!' Becca said. It was almost a yell. 'We can't just sit here and do nothing. I don't know why we agreed to Doug's stupid plan. He could be dead already. The forecast is for thick cloud from eleven. Maybe they are waiting for it to get really dark before they take his body and sling it over the cliffs. He's my baby's father. I am not going to sit and wait any longer.'

'We have to adapt,' Laura said.

'We have to do something!' Becca was a woman on the verge.

'We need to stick together,' Zoe interrupted, with surprising calmness. 'I suggest you come back, Laura, and pick us up, and then we will agree a plan. Doug said we should stick together, otherwise the plan will never work.'

'I agree,' Becca said, louder than ever. 'Come and get us, Laura, and while you do I'm going to ring DI Jennings.'

'OK, keep calm,' Laura snapped. 'I'm on my way now.'

'Is this the rendezvous place?' Doug said. He didn't want to provoke the guy, but if he could distract him that could only be good. The man stayed silent, except for his fingers which began to drum on the steering wheel.

'And what is the new plan? Because my plan was that I would be given a nice wedge of cash and then I would drive off into the sunset never to be seen again.'

'If you believe that, you really are a dipstick!'

'Or is the new plan to push me over the nearest convenient cliff? If so, why are we still sitting here? Why don't you get on and do it? Of course, the chances are the police will think it's a bit of a coincidence if I end up at the bottom of a cliff like Josie – especially when I have been making such a fuss about her and Layla. So they will very definitely investigate and the chances are they will find your DNA on me, or at least my DNA all over your van, and in that case you will become the fall guy.'

'Shut it, dipstick, or I'll give you and your mutt a taste of my baseball bat.'

'Dipstick? That's what you called me the day you, Joshua and Matt attacked me. It's a bit of a giveaway if you were hoping I wouldn't know who you are. As for beating me to death with a baseball bat, do you really think that is the way to win Roxanne's favour after all this time? Killing the one person who is determined to discover the truth about her daughter's death?'

This time there was no 'shut it' from him. Just silence. Stunned silence – Doug hoped.

'Frank, you are one of the few people I know didn't kill Layla because you were in bed with her mother at the time of her death. What was it, the third time? That's what Roxanne told me. But that night was the end of it.'

'Please!' Frank said. 'Just leave it. I'm just the delivery man, making sure it isn't a set up, that there aren't hordes of police watching.'

'The problem with being the delivery man, Frank, is that it's you who cops it if things go wrong.'

'You've asked for a meeting and that's what you're going to get. And that is all I know.'

Doug said nothing. He felt sorry for the man.

There was a sudden hooting as a car went past.

'Bloody hell,' Frank said. 'It's that bitch again, in her convertible, heading back to Bude. She even had the nerve to flash her headlights at me – and hoot.'

'Perhaps she fancies you?' Doug said pushing his luck again. And perhaps he would have copped more than another 'shut it' if Frank's mobile hadn't rung at that moment. He answered it.

'All clear,' he said.

Then: 'Another one?'

Then: 'See you there.'

He started the engine. 'Hold tight. Another change of plan.'

The silver convertible shot down the hill into Bude much faster than it should have done, slowed suddenly with a squeal of rubber and turned smartly into a short driveway in Lynstone Road. Laura was out of the car almost before the engine had stopped. Moments later she was banging on the front door of the house.

She had hoped the two women would have calmed down, but as soon as Becca opened the door, it was immediately obvious that her stress levels had gone up several notches.

'They're on the move,' she wailed. 'And we've lost the dog-tracker signal. They must be out of range.'

'Were they still heading south-west?'

'As far as we can tell.' Zoe spoke calmly. She had decided that Becca, who had been such a wonderful support to her up until this crisis, was in the middle of cracking up altogether.

'I tried ringing Jennings,' Becca wailed, 'but she's not answering. I've left a message, but why on earth isn't she answering?'

Laura could think of various possibilities, but didn't see the point of listing them. Instead she laid her hands on Becca's shoulders and looked her deep in the face. 'I am going to go and follow that van. I know what it looks like, we know what general direction it is going in and if we get closer the dog-tracker should kick in again. You stay here.' She placed her hand on Becca's bump. 'The fact is that you have a lot to lose, and I have nothing.'

'I lost everything a long time ago,' another voice said.

The three of them turned to see a woman standing at the door, a set of keys dangling in her hand.'

'Roxanne!' Becca looked at her in amazement.

'What colour is the van?'

'White,' Laura said. 'Tinted windows. Doug Mullen is in it. With his dog. He's in danger and—'

'Do you know the registration number?'

Laura told her.

'That's Frank's van. Where are they?'

'Along the coast. Doug was trying to arrange a meet up, but it's gone wrong.'

'In that case we'd better go and rescue him. Have you got room for me?'

'Sure,' Laura said.

'I'm coming too,' Zoe said. 'I have a pepper spray and a knife. And I've learnt how to use them.'

'Leave the knife,' Roxanne said. 'We use our tongues as our weapons. And our numbers.

'Let's go.' Laura was heading for the door. 'There's no time to waste.'

Zoe and Roxanne followed. And so did Becca. *Stick together.* That was what Doug had said. *Whatever you do.* She had made a promise, and she wasn't going to break it now.

Doug started to count. Whether it would be any use he rather doubted, but it gave him a focus. By the time he had got to 250, the van was climbing, and not too smoothly. They were headed for somewhere less busy. He reckoned that typically there would be quite a few people who used the Bude to Widemouth Bay road at night, so a bad place for whatever it was the guys had in mind. He tried to slow his breathing down and stay focused. The one good thing was that he had made some sort of progress with Frank, stirred up doubts in his mind and maybe make him reluctant to go along with the others.

He had got to 473 when Frank let out a sigh of relief. 'Ah, there they are.' He swung the van to the right and into another bumpy stopping place. This was high up, Doug reckoned. Much higher than the previous one, but still on the coast road. He was pretty sure they hadn't turned inland.

'Get him out,' someone said. Almost certainly Gooch, Doug decided. No surprise there. 'And, hellfire, why have you brought his dog? Leave him in the van. We don't want him snapping at our heels. And when you've done that follow me.'

Someone, presumably Frank, took his arm and steered him along a rough and uncertain path. He stumbled a couple of times, and each time the hand gripped harder and pulled him back upright. Other feet crunched in front, and a squeaking of wheels made Doug realise that Andy Trent was there too in his wheelchair. He felt pleased about that. Was Joshua there too? He did hope so. That would make it a full house.

Laura drove up the hill like a bat out of hell, albeit a very noisy bat. She had no plans beyond getting there before it was too late, before Doug Mullen … She tried not to continue that line of thinking. When she had asked him how she could help him nail Gooch, and when he had put forward his plan, her first thought was that he had gone stark staring bonkers. She had thought he was playing right into their hands. And yet by the time he had waved her goodbye, she had promised him that she would be with him all the way. There was no way she was going to miss out on getting justice – and revenge.

She dropped a gear and swerved past an electric cyclist who had himself swerved to avoid a pothole.

Focus, she told herself.

'Crashing won't help our cause,' Roxanne said, her voice firm and surprisingly prissy.

'I'm monitoring the dog tracker,' Zoe said from the back. 'But there's no signal yet.'

When they reached Widemouth Bay, Laura braked hard and pulled into the parking area where the white van had been. She shone her torch around, in case anything had been dropped, but within thirty seconds she had given up and was back in the car.

'There's a left turn in a few hundred metres,' Zoe said.

'Don't take it,' Becca replied. 'The chances are that the rendezvous will be on the cliffs.' She spoke calmly, her earlier emotional panic banished to some locked room at the back of her brain. No-one asked her why she thought the rendezvous would be 'on the cliffs' because they knew the answer all too well.

Laura drove as fast as she safely could, and very soon afterwards Zoe was piping up from the back again. 'In half a mile, near Widemouth Manor, we could follow the road, but it swings left towards the Atlantic Highway. Otherwise there's a right turn that stays much closer to the coast.'

'Right,' the others said in unison.

Laura, was soon dropping down into fourth gear as she pushed hard up the steepish gradient of the minor road.

Zoe squealed in excitement. 'Got the dog, got the dog! Keep going. It's less than a mile away.'

'Count the distance down,' Laura said. She could feel the tension building in her. This was going to be her chance to nail Gooch. One way or another, this was going to be her chance to gain justice and revenge for her father. 'I'm going to kill the lights before we get there. We walk the last bit.'

Doug was feeling disoriented. He guessed they were heading towards the cliffs. He tried to prepare himself for whatever was in store for him. The good news was that he was still alive. If the intention had been a swift execution job, he would have been dead by now. Which meant that Gooch, or whoever it was who was calling the shots, wanted to know how much he knew, and what evidence he had, and then assess whether they could safely pay him off or push himself over the edge. Frank, he felt certain, was not somcone who would happily commit murder. He was the stooge, helping the others because he always had and because he had no idea who had killed Layla. If he had, given his feelings for Roxanne, he would surely never have sat quiet all these years and done nothing.

They came to a halt.

'You can go now,' someone ordered.

'I don't want to.' That was Frank's voice, immediately to Doug's left. He was still holding him by the arm.

'This is nothing to do with you, you've done me a favour, now go home and forget all about it.'

There was a sudden noise in the darkness, and something small and furry ran up and jumped up against Doug's legs. He bent down and hugged him.

'How the hell has he got out the van? Can't you even do a simple job like that?'

'Someone must have let him out.'

'You bonehead. Have they tailed you?'

'There's a transmitter in the dog's collar,' Doug said through his hood. 'He wasn't to know.'

'You absolute idiot.'

'What are you going to do to Mullen?' Frank demanded.

'Just go, man. Or you'll be implicated.'

'He knows who I am.' Doug felt Frank release his arm and then his hood was being wrenched off. It took a few moments for his eyes to adjust, but when they did, he saw Frank had pulled his own mask off and was pointing at Gooch. Andy and Joshua Trent were watching in stunned silence.

'I want to know what happened to Layla,' Frank demanded.

'Mick Raglan killed her. Everyone knows that. Josie saw them together. When we searched the sea pool, we found Mick's bracelet there. He must have tried it on with her. She resisted and he killed her. Case closed. Now clear off, Frank.'

'He's not clearing off anywhere.' The voice was female and authoritative. Gooch turned to see Roxanne Lark standing there, and behind her three others.

'What the hell is going on?'

'Let me introduce Zoe Finn, though you may remember her by her childhood name of Jennie Raglan. And do you remember Laura Duke, Danny's daughter? And this is Becca Baines, who did her best to look after Naomi, though for some reason the Trents weren't too happy for her to do so.'

Gooch said nothing for several seconds. Then: 'I am here only because Mr Mullen asked for a meeting. He wanted me to pay him off. Then he said he would clear off and stop stirring up trouble and spouting lies. Candice Kipling will vouch for that. Mullen is a liar and a charlatan.'

Laura stepped forward and stood right next to Roxanne. 'I found a letter from Mick Raglan in my dad's possessions. He insisted that he was innocent. That he had been fitted up. He begged my father to re-examine the case. I think he started to. I think he may even have realised that you, Detective Sergeant Gooch, planted Mick's bracelet in the sea pool that first morning, when he was away on a training course and you were the officer in charge.'

'And how would I have got hold of Mick's bracelet?'

'Perhaps I can answer that,' Doug said. 'It's only a theory, of course, but it kind of makes sense. Mick had an affair with Judy Trent. I know that for a fact. Only problem was, he took his bracelet off in the bedroom – it was a present from his wife and he was probably ashamed to be wearing it while sleeping with Judy. Andy must have found it.'

'What the hell are you talking about?' Andy said. 'Judy would never—'

'Oh, but she did. You know she did. Mick admitted to me that he had an affair with Judy. Not a long one, but it was fatal for him. When Layla died, Josie and Naomi heard about it and of course they went down to the sea pool to see if their friend really was dead. That was when Josie told the police that she had seen Mick with Layla. And of course Andy still had the bracelet, so he had the perfect evidence to nail the man who had slept with his wife and who he believed had killed Layla. Planting it in the pool with the police and crime scene team there was impossible for him, but not for his mate DS Gooch. You and Goochie go back a long way, don't you, Andy, so a nod and a wink and mum's the word and the bracelet ends up at the bottom of the sea pool where the crime scene guys find it. By the time Danny appears the next day, the case was pretty much solved.'

'So who did kill my daughter, Doug?' Roxanne wailed.

'Now that I don't know,' Doug said. 'But one of the Trent family obviously.'

'Why obviously?' Andy Trent pushed himself forward. 'I admit you got it right about Mick's bracelet.'

'Don't say anything, Andy,' Gooch said.

'Why? I am happy to admit I gave you the bracelet to put in the sea pool. I did so with the best of intentions, to make sure a murderer was convicted and put away.'

'Or was that to protect yourself, Andy? Perhaps it was you who killed Layla.'

'Of course not. Why would I have?'

'To protect one of your family.'

'What are you talking about?'

'The question is why would anyone have killed Layla. What links Layla and your family? Naomi, obviously. They were best buddies.' Doug turned away from Andy. 'But there was another connection … wasn't there, Joshua? You.'

'You're talking rubbish.'

'You had an affair with Layla.'

'What do you mean? You're making this up. I would never have slept with that slut.'

'Oh, but you did. Naomi told me so. She came in and caught you at it. And soon after that you split up. Naomi insisted to me that it was amicable, but was it really?'

'Frank,' Gooch called. 'Get the cuffs off Mullen. This meeting has finished. We are not saying another word. We are all going home.'

Frank removed the cuffs, but otherwise no-one moved.

Doug pressed on. 'I doubt it was amicable. Joshua, you were one of the rising rugby stars of Bude, barely eighteen but already in the first team, and you were being cast off by Layla, who could have her pick of men and liked to play them off one against another.'

'I didn't kill her,' Joshua said. 'I didn't, I didn't.' His breath was coming in great gulps. 'Layla and I … we agreed it wasn't working.'

'Not working? You just described her as a slut. Not working? Why would you call her a slut if your parting was so amicable?'

'I did not kill her.' For a moment, Doug thought that Joshua was going to cry, but he pulled himself back from the brink. 'You've got to believe me.'

Doug paused. 'Well, I think I maybe do believe you, Joshua. But if that is the case, it leaves us with two possibilities. I am sorry to say that those are either your mother Judy, or your sister Naomi. Because I suspect that both of them hated Layla for the way she had treated you. They both thought she was a slut. And one of them killed her for it. And I expect your father knows which one it was.'

'I've heard enough,' Andy Trent snarled into the darkness, and then began to wheel himself furiously down the track towards the parking area. 'I'm going.'

'No you are not.'

The four women stepped smartly in front of him

like a highly trained dance troupe.

'The police are on their way,' Laura said. And as if to underline the fact, there was the distant sound of blues and twos, and moments after that the flashing lights of a convoy of police vehicles emerged out of the darkness.

'You bastard!' The explosion of anger came out of the dark. Frank ran straight at Gooch and brought him crashing to the ground with a rugby tackle straight out of the 'how to knock 'em to the ground so hard they don't get up' rulebook.

Doug ran forward to intervene. Given the state of his ribs and the strength of Frank, this was not the smartest move, and he might have paid for it with a few more broken ribs if a high-pitched scream from just behind his left shoulder had not brought Frank to his senses.

'Stop, Frank. That's enough. It won't bring Layla back.'

He froze, and moments later Roxanne had grabbed his arm and pulled him away like a mother separating two squabbling boys.

The next couple of minutes were chaos as police descended on the scene, shouting and waving torches and grabbing every man there except for Doug.

Jennings made her way to Gooch, who was being handcuffed by Bristow and a police constable she recognised, but whose name had temporarily escaped her.

'Read him his rights, Sergeant.'

'It wasn't me,' Gooch said. 'I thought it was Mick Raglan. That's why we arrested him. What with Josie seeing him talking to Layla and then finding his bracelet in the sea pool, it was a no brainer.'

'Read him his rights,' Jennings repeated, 'and take him away.'

She turned away and walked over to Doug Mullen, who was standing surrounded by his cortege of women. He had his dog tucked under his arm.

'How are you feeling?' she asked.

'Glad it's over,' he said.

'I think you've probably earned a nice holiday.'

'You'll be wanting a statement.'

'A formal interview, in due course.'

'So who did kill my daughter?' Roxanne said, looking first at Jennings and then at Doug.

There was silence. Roxanne looked around and her face fell as the truth began to dawn on her.

'Doug, tell us,' Becca said. 'Put us out of our misery. For Zoe's and Roxanne's sake, tell us you know.'

'Ma'am!' It was DS Bristow striding towards them. He was puffing and wheezing.

'Can't it wait for a minute, Chris. I am busy.'

'Don't think so, ma'am.'

'So what is it?'

'It's Joshua Trent, ma'am. He says he wants to confess.'

'I want to tell you all exactly where things stand.' DI Jennings looked around the room. Roxanne Lark, Zoe Finch, Laura Duke, Doug Mullen and Becca Baines were scattered round the room in armchairs and a three-seater sofa, and they were watching her on high alert. Even the dog was sitting on Doug's knees, upright and alert, as if the DI might at any moment toss him a doggie treat or a ball to chase.

'Joshua Trent has confessed to the killing of Layla Lark and Josie Archer. We have now received a complete report on the forensics of Josie, and the details tie up. In particular, examination of Joshua's footwear and analysis of the cliff confirms that it was indeed him who pushed her off the cliff, and a scratch on her wrist matches Joshua's DNA.

'Andy Trent admits to giving Mick Raglan's bracelet to Jim Gooch, and Gooch admits that he slipped it into the sea pool, but both insist they did it because they believed that Mick Raglan was guilty and they wanted to make sure he was convicted.'

'Bastards!' Zoe said.

Jennings paused and looked at Zoe. 'I agree, Zoe. Their actions have resulted in an innocent man being imprisoned, so they will face a trial and no doubt a significant sentence. They will not escape justice, although that will not change the injustice that your father has suffered.'

She paused again, and waited as Becca gave Zoe a tissue, and then slipped her arm round her slight body.

'Did Gooch say anything about my father?' Laura was sitting stiffly in her armchair, hands clasped.

'He admits nothing. We have instigated a search of his house, and we found a letter which he too received from Raglan at the same time as your father did, and almost identical in its wording. We also found an unlicensed gun in his wardrobe, but of course neither of those things prove anything.'

Silence descended. After a respectful pause Jennings asked if there were any questions.

'Yes.' Doug scratched at his shaven chin. 'Did Joshua say why he killed Josie?'

'Oh, yes. He said he killed her because she was party to the killing of Layla. After you had come to Bude and started questioning her, she got into a complete panic that they would be caught. They met on the cliffs and he pushed her over, though only after a struggle in which he scratched her.'

'But why would she have been party to Layla's killing? What was her motive?'

'Jealousy, according to Joshua. Apparently Layla stole Josie's boyfriend from her. So she and Joshua got together and decided, as Joshua said, to have it out with Layla. He said Josie hit her with a large stone, and he claims he pushed her into the pool thinking she was already dead. I think his lawyers will do their best to play on that, but the autopsy proved long ago that Layla died from drowning, not from the blow to the head.'

'So,' said Doug, 'let me get this straight. In court his lawyers will very likely argue that in the case of Layla, his part in her murder was unintended, and in the case of Josie they had a scuffle on the edge of the cliffs and she accidentally fell, and he will plead contrition and throw himself on the mercy of the court.'

Jennings nodded. 'I guess so.'

'How do we know he isn't protecting someone?'

'I'm not with you, Doug.'

'Andy has confessed to his part in framing Mick

Raglan, but will argue that he only did it because he was convinced that Mick was the killer. Josie had seen them together at the bus stop. So we have both Andy and Joshua both pleading guilty, but with mitigating circumstances. They'll get sentenced, but how long will they actually be in prison?'

Jennings stood up. 'That's not for us to decide,' she said, suddenly prissy, and clearly very tired.

'Space control to Major Mullen!'

Doug turned to look at Becca, a look of blank incomprehension on his face.

'You what?'

'You're not exactly a barrel of laughs. You have dragged me all the way here and said barely a word.'

'All the way here' was something of an exaggeration. They were sitting on a bench by the canal where the fishermen tended to gather, but Becca was feeling irritable because the need to head to the nearest toilet was rising inexorably through her.

'Sorry,' he said.

'So what is going on inside your head?'

'I think she got away with it.'

'She?'

'I don't think Josie was involved in Layla's death – apart from the fact that she saw Raglan at the bus stop.'

'So who is "she"?'

'Not Naomi. I did wonder about her, but having seen her close up, I can't believe it was her. She was genuinely frightened and confused when she came to us.'

'Who then?'

'Judy Trent.'

Becca was stunned. 'Are you serious?'

'Andy and Joshua are covering for her.' Doug's eyes were no longer on Becca, but on a heron flying serenely from right to left up above the grassy hillside opposite. 'She put up with Andy for years – drunkenness, a disabling crash, and prison. She put up with all of that. But what she could not put up with was Layla playing fast and loose with her darling son.'

Becca sat back on the bench and tried to process what he had said. She just wanted this episode of their life to be over. For Doug to put this case behind him. For them to get back home so they could focus together on the baby growing inside her and for the future which lay before them.

'Can you prove it?'

'No.'

'And if Judy was involved in Layla's murder, did she also kill Josie Archer?'

'Oh no! I think the forensics make it clear that Joshua killed her. And he killed her not because she saw Mick Raglan, but because Josie saw something else. My guess is that she saw Joshua and his mother shortly after that. Of course, she never reported it because she was never asked the right question, and it never occurred to her that seeing Joshua and his mother taking a walk in the area was in any way relevant. That next morning when she and Naomi went down to the sea pool to see if their friend really was dead, she told the police that she had seen Layla with Mick, because she had. Within hours Mick's bracelet turns up on the bottom of the sea pool, and after that it was inevitable that he was arrested for murder.'

Becca took his hand in hers and squeezed it, but he carried on oblivious to it. 'It might have been days, months or even years before Josie began to suspect the truth. Maybe it was only when I turned up asking my questions that she began to put two and two together. Presumably when they met on the cliff, she said something to Joshua about seeing him and his mother that night. They argued, it got out of control, and he used his strength to push her over the cliff and shut her up. If I hadn't questioned her, if I hadn't come and started asking questions, Josie might still be alive.'

'Doug Mullen,' she snapped. 'You have rescued Roxanne and Zoe from their misery. You have given Laura Duke something to cling on to. You have done your best.'

'I suppose so.'

'There's no supposing about it.'

He looked at her. A half smile creased his face, and he stared into hers as if he was seeing it for the first time. 'And you *are* the best!'

'I am not the best. I am merely she who must be obeyed. I order you now to give me a kiss – a proper kiss, mind you, not one of your half-baked ones – and after that you must escort me gallantly to the toilets before I have an accident.'

THE END

ABOUT THE AUTHOR

Peter Tickler has lived the majority of his life in Oxford. He read classics at Keble College, then returned to the city a few years later to raise his family there. So when he decided to write a crime novel, it was almost inevitable that he would set it in Oxford – though 'town' rather than 'gown'.

His own unusual surname, and the part his great-grandfather played in the First World War as manufacturer of jam for the British troops on the front line, finally caused a change of direction in his writing. It took him back to Lincolnshire, where he grew up, and to the year 1919, a time of upheaval and re-evaluation for those who survived the fighting.

Death in the Sea Pool evolved gradually, the result of many off-season holidays in the village of Maramchurch, two miles from Bude.

ALSO BY
PETER TICKLER

Blood in Oxford Series
Blood on the Cowley Road
Blood in Grandpont
Blood on the Marsh

Standalone
The Tickler's Jam Murders
The Girl Who Stole the Apple

Doug Mullen – Private Detective
Dead in the Water
White Lies, Deadly Lies
Dead in Oxford
The Oxford Murders

Printed in Dunstable, United Kingdom